PRAISE FOR AFRAID OF THE CHRISTMAS LIGHTS

'Stellar'
The Guardian

'Enjoyable'
The Observer

'Haunting'
The Times

'The biggest stars in contemporary crime fiction'
The Sunday Record

'Cracking...All the stories are truly gripping'
My Weekly

'This anthology is a bulging stocking full of prize gifts. Funny, tragic, scary and clever- the perfect Christmas present'
Louise Beech

'A wicked slay-ride through the dark days of Winter'
Trevor Wood

'Twisted, devious, delicious. If you're looking for a

mystery in your Christmas stocking, this collection of crime tales will be right up your candy-cane lane'
Jo Spain

'A perfect festive collection of bite-sized crime fiction. I thoroughly enjoyed every last morsel'
John Marrs

'A deliciously dark selection pack of stories you'll devour'
Sarah Pinborough

AFRAID OF THE CHRISTMAS LIGHTS

Foreword by Val McDermid
Edited and compiled by Miranda Jewess and Victoria Selman

Mark Billingham
Rachael Blok
Heather Critchlow
Elle Croft
James Delargy
Clare Empson
Jo Furniss
Sophie Hannah
T.E. Kinsey
N.J. Mackay
S.R. Masters
Phoebe Morgan
Dominic Nolan
Robert Scragg

Victoria Selman
Kate Simants
Adam Southward
Harriet Tyce

CHARITIES

All profits from the sale of this anthology will be donated to East Surrey Domestic Abuse Services and Rights of Women.

East Surrey Domestic Abuse Services (ESDAS) is an independent charity providing outreach and associated services in the borough of Reigate & Banstead and the districts of Mole Valley and Tandridge. ESDAS is dedicated to educating professionals, communities and victims to enable them to protect themselves and those around them, and to helping victims at the moment of maximum danger when they attempt to leave their abusers. You can call them on 01737 771350, text on 07860 039720, make a referral by emailing leigh.esdas@esdas.cjsm.net, or visit their website: www.esdas.org.uk.

Rights of Women is a charity set up to help women suffering from domestic violence understand their legal rights and how the law can help them. 'We believe that women need this advice and information to enable them to make safe and informed choices for themselves and their families.' Call them on 020 7251 6577, email info@row.org.uk, or visit their website: www.rightsofwomen.org.uk.

In memory of John Marshall aka John Sessions
1953-2020

'There are some people who want to throw their arms round you simply because it is Christmas; there are other people who want to strangle you simply because it is Christmas.'

ROBERT WILSON LYND

CONTENTS

CONTRIBUTORS

Underneath the Mistletoe Last Night Mark Billingham

The Breadwinner Sophie Hannah

Bad Guy Kate Simants

An Unexpected Present Phoebe Morgan

Just Kids S.R. Masters

Especially at Christmas Adam Southward

The Bedminster Bird Burglaries T.E. Kinsey

Fresh Meat Elle Croft

Heavenly Peace Heather Critchlow

The Switch James Delargy

Secret Santa Jo Furniss

A Dog is for Life, Not Just for Christmas Robert Scragg

Driving Home for Christmas Rachael Blok

Smithereens Dominic Nolan

FOREWORD

The trouble with being invited to write the foreword to an anthology is that it can turn into a very expensive business. Of course, there will be writers with whose backlist one is familiar, who offer no new plums to be plucked from the pudding. But there will also be fresh meat for the hungry reader; writers earlier in their career than the old favourites, writers whose short fiction promises delights, writers who draw us to the booksellers so we can feed our habit with our credit cards.

And so it was for me with *Afraid of the Christmas Lights*. The TBR pile has grown higher as a result... And I can safely promise that you'll have the same response. There are stories here to suit everyone, from the darkest of noir to the lightest of festive touches. And the joy of Christmas is that you can share the delight by giving it as a gift to all the readers in your life – even the casual ones, because who doesn't love a short story every now and then?

There's an added bonus with this particular anthology. It comes with the added glow of virtue because the profits will be donated to ESDAS (www.esdas.org.uk) and Rights of Women (www.rightsofwomen.org.uk), charities that provide support for victims of domestic abuse. It's particularly relevant in these difficult days; lockdown in its various forms means that many victims have no hiding place from their abusers. There is already compelling evidence that levels of domestic abuse have risen significantly since COVID-19 restrictions were first imposed. As the recent advertising campaign has it, 'Domestic abusers always work from home.' Charities like ESDAS are struggling to keep up with the calls on their services. Whatever support we can provide is vital.

This Christmas will be dramatically different for most of us from our Christmases past. But the comfort of reading is a constant. It's a salve for isolation and a haven when we need to escape into someone else's imagination. I hope you enjoy these Christmas bonbons as much as I have.

Take care and stay safe over the festive period.

Val McDermid
Christmas 2020

UNDERNEATH THE MISTLETOE LAST NIGHT

Mark Billingham

Jack knew all about 'being good for goodness sake'. He'd heard it in that song, but he didn't think opening his presents a few hours early would count as being bad. Besides, he had been asleep and even if it was still dark outside, it was already Christmas Day, so it wasn't really cheating, was it?

He lay awake a few minutes longer, wondering if it was snowing outside. If Rudolph shared that carrot they had left for him with all the other reindeer and if the elves were already working on the toys for next year. He tried thinking about all sorts of things, but he couldn't keep his mind off those shiny parcels under the tree downstairs.

He climbed out of bed.

He decided that bare feet would be quieter, so ignoring the Sam-7 slippers at the foot of his bed, he crept slowly out of his room and downstairs. He took one step at a time, wincing at every creak. The door to the living room was open, so he could see the tree before he reached the bottom of the stairs.

He could see what was lying underneath it. *Who...*

The red of his coat and the white of his thick beard. The shiny black belt and boots. Not as fat as Jack had been expecting, but maybe he was on a diet.

He waited for a minute at the foot of the stairs, then padded softly into the living room. He had always thought it must be very tiring. All those houses to visit in one night. If Father Christmas chose this particular house to have a nap in, did that mean other children would not be getting their presents? Or was this the last house on his journey?

Jack crept a little closer, then stopped. He let out a small gasp and clamped a hand across his mouth. He watched and waited for the chest to move, to hear a breath or a snuffle, but he could hear nothing but the low hum of the fridge in the kitchen and a strange hiss inside in his own head.

One arm was lying funny.

A crinkled boot was half on and half off.

A different sort of red, where it shouldn't have been.

The boy turned and bolted up the stairs. He charged into his parents' room, shouting for his mum. She sat up and blinked and he ran to her, breathless, fighting to get the words out.

'Somebody killed Father Christmas...'

◆ ◆ ◆

Tom Thorne had not needed to think very long before signing himself up for the Christmas Day shift. It made no real difference to him. There was no family to spend it with and, far as he was concerned, Christmas Day was as good or bad a day to die as any other.

None of his regular team was at the house when he arrived, and clambering into the plastic bodysuit in the small front garden, he exchanged cursory nods of recognition or understanding with those officers already there.

We're the sad buggers. The ones with no lives.

Through a gaggle of SOCOs and police photographers, he was relieved to see the familiar figure of Phil Hendricks crouched over the body. The pathologist had been dumped by his partner a few weeks previously and he and Thorne had already agreed to have Christmas lunch together at a local pub if no calls came in. Now, it looked like they would have to settle for turkey sandwiches and a few beers at Thorne's flat.

'This is a strange one,' Hendricks said.

Thorne thought, *They're the ones I like best*, but just nodded.

'Who the hell would want to do Santa in?' The pathologist laid a gloved finger against the dead man's face. 'The tooth fairy? Jack Frost...?'

'I'm keeping an open mind,' Thorne said. 'What are we looking at?'

'Single stab wound, far as I can see.'

'Knife?'

A DC Thorne did not know appeared behind him. 'No sign of it,' he said. He nodded back towards the kitchen. 'Broken window at the back and sod all under the tree except our friend here. Pretty obvious he disturbed a burglar...'

Thorne had to concede that it looked that way. Easy pickings for thieves on Christmas Eve. People out celebrating and a healthy selection of must-have gadgets sitting under trees in nine out of ten living rooms. 'Where's the wife?' he asked.

'Upstairs,' the DC said. 'Family Liaison Officer's with her.'

'What about the boy?'

'A car's taking him to his mum's parents.'

Thorne nodded.

'By all accounts the kid didn't get a good look, so he doesn't know... you know. Not yet, anyway.'

Thorne watched as the funeral directors came into the room. They unzipped the body bag and knelt beside the dead man, which Thorne took as his cue to go upstairs and meet the widow.

◆ ◆ ◆

Wendy Fielding sat on the edge of the bed, a female Family

Liaison Officer next to her. Each cradled a mug of tea. *Always tea*, Thorne thought, wondering why the Murder Squad was not looking towards Tetley for some sort of sponsorship. He told the FLO to step outside, asked Mrs Fielding if she felt up to talking. She nodded and Thorne sat down on a large wooden trunk against the wall.

'I'm sorry for your loss,' he said. The room was dimly lit by a bedside lamp, but the first milky slivers of morning light were creeping through a gap in the curtains.

She said, 'Thank you' and tried to smile. She was in her late thirties, Thorne guessed, though for obvious reasons she looked a little older. She wore a powder-blue housecoat, but when she shifted on the bed, Thorne could see that the front of the pale nightdress beneath was soaked with blood.

'Can you take me through what happened this morning?' Thorne asked.

She nodded without raising her head and took a deep breath. 'It was just after one o'clock,' she said. 'I know because I looked at the clock when Jack came in.' She spoke quietly and quickly, as though worried that, were she to hesitate even for a second, she might fall apart. 'He told me that Father Christmas was dead... that someone had killed him in the living room. I told him to stay here... I tucked him up in bed and...' Then there was hesitation, and Thorne watched her swallow hard. She looked up at him. 'He doesn't know it's his dad. He still believes in...' She puffed out her cheeks, swallowed again. 'When do you think I should tell him?'

'We'll put you in touch with bereavement counsellors,' Thorne told her. 'They'll be able to advise you.'

'Right,' she said.

Thorne thought he could smell booze on her, but said nothing. He could hardly blame the woman for needing a stiff drink to go with her tea.

'Tell me about the Santa outfit,' he said.

Another attempt at a smile. 'Alan had been planning it for ages,' she said. 'It was his office party last night and they always have a Father Christmas, so he decided he was going to bring the costume home then dress up in it to take Jack's presents up. He pretends to be asleep, you know? You got kids?'

Thorne shook his head.

'Alan thought it would be special, you know? If Jack saw Father Christmas putting the presents at the end of his bed.'

'So you went downstairs?'

'He was just lying there, like Jack said he was. I knelt down and picked him up, but I knew he'd gone. There was so much blood on his chest and coming out of his mouth... sorry.'

'Take a minute,' Thorne said.

'It's fine. I'm fine.'

'Did you hear anything before that?' Thorne asked. 'The glass in the back door breaking? Somebody moving about downstairs?'

'I'm a heavy sleeper,' she said. 'I was dead to the world until Jack came in.'

Thorne nodded, wondering if the alcohol he could smell had actually been drunk the night before.

'So, you think they were in the house when Alan came home?'

'We're still working downstairs,' Thorne said. 'But if he disturbed a burglar that would mean he was already wearing the costume, which seems a bit odd.'

'Maybe he changed into it at the party.'

'Maybe,' Thorne said.

They both turned at the soft knock and turned to see the Detective Constable standing awkwardly in the doorway.

'Something you need to see,' he said.

◆ ◆ ◆

Thorne got down on his belly to peer beneath the tree and saw a mobile phone sitting hard against the skirting board. He gave the officer the nod and the man crawled under the tree, his plastic bodysuit snagging on the branches as he stretched to reach the phone. Having retrieved the handset, he handed it across to Thorne, who almost dropped it when it began to ring in his hand. Everyone in the room froze.

'Write the number down,' he barked.

The DC scrabbled for pen and notebook and scribbled down the number on the phone's display. They waited for the phone to stop ringing, then heard the alert that told them a message had been left.

'Shall we?' Thorne asked.

The DC held his notebook out so that Thorne could read the number and Thorne dialled.

A woman answered. She said, 'Hello,' and when Thorne began to introduce himself, she hung up.

'Get on to the phone company,' Thorne said.

'Our burglar dropped his phone, you reckon?' Hendricks asked. 'Looks like you might have got yourself an early Christmas present.'

'I was hoping for an iPad,' Thorne said.

◆ ◆ ◆

Bright and early on a freezing Boxing Day and Thorne was standing in a Forensic Science Service lab next to a balding technician named Turnbull. Thorne knew the man was recently divorced. Another sad case who preferred working to sitting at home alone and wondering if his kids were having a good day.

'What have we got?'

'Two text messages,' Turnbull said, pointing to the phone. '7.37 on Christmas Eve and again half an hour later. Plus the voice message that was left when you were at the murder scene.'

Thorne had already established when Alan Fielding had left home to go to his firm's Christmas party. One message had been sent just before he left and the second would have arrived when he was on his way there.

'Let's see,' Thorne said.

Turnbull handed him a transcript of the messages.

19.37. 24/12/11. It's me. Just wondered if you'd left yet. I'm guessing ur having trouble getting away. Can't wait to see u. x

Then...

19.54. 24/12/11. Hope ur on your way. Hurry up and get here will u? Can't wait to give u yr Xmas present. I know ur going to like it. X

And last, a transcript of the voice message, left in the early hours of Christmas morning.

'Just me. Couldn't sleep. Tonight was amazing though. I know you can't tell her today... I'm not expecting you to, but do it soon, OK? Oh, and you're the sexiest Santa I've ever seen...'

'So, what do you think?' Turnbull asked.

Thorne stared at the phone. He already knew who the messages were from. The same woman who had called the phone found underneath the Christmas tree; the phone they thought had been left by whoever had killed Alan Fielding. Thorne now knew that the phone was Fielding's, that he had forgotten to take it with him, and that the caller was Angela Massey, a twenty-four-year-old secretary who worked at the same company as he did.

Thorne had spoken to her on Christmas Day, just before the umpteenth repeat of *The Great Escape*. He was due to interview her formally later that day.

He blinked slowly. His head was still thick after the night before, when he and Hendricks had drunk far too much and swapped distinctly unseasonal banter.

'Knife went straight through his heart,' Hendricks had said. 'Probably dead before he hit the deck.'

'Something, I suppose.'

'Not the best way to round off Christmas Eve.'

'Yeah, well...'

'What?'

'I think he'd had quite a good night up to that point.'

'So, that help you?' Turnbull asked. 'The stuff on the phone?'

'Yeah that helps,' Thorne said. 'Helps me screw up Christmas for at least a couple more people.'

◆ ◆ ◆

'I need to get Jack from my mum's, so can we just get this over with?' Wendy Fielding shifted in her seat, bit down on her bottom lip. 'I haven't told him yet, but he's been asking questions about his dad.' She looked down at the scarred metal tabletop. 'My mum told him that Alan had to go on a business trip.'

'This shouldn't take long,' Thorne said.

Though concessions had been made to the season elsewhere in the station—a few strings of tinsel in the canteen, an ironic sprig of mistletoe in the custody suite—the interview room was as bland and bare as it was for the rest of the year. Thorne turned on the twin CD recorders, and pointed to the camera high on the wall to let Wendy Fielding know that their interview was being recorded.

'I don't understand,' she said. 'I thought you just wanted a chat.'

'Where are the presents, Wendy?'

She looked at him. 'How the hell should I know? Thieving bastard sold them for drugs, most likely. That's what they do, isn't it?'

'Some of them,' Thorne said.

'I don't know how they live with themselves.' She shook her head, disgusted, but she would not meet Thorne's eyes.

'You're right, of course,' Thorne said. 'Our burglar would probably have sold your son's Christmas presents for a few wraps of heroin. If he'd existed.'

Now she looked, eyes wide.

'I'm guessing you stashed them up in the loft or somewhere. Along with the knife. That might have been before or after you broke the window in the back door. Doesn't really matter.'

'What are you talking about? I think you're the one on drugs.'

'You really should have thought about the phone though. The one you chucked at your husband. It was the phone that made us think we might catch our burglar, but what was on it told me there wasn't a burglar to catch.' Thorne glanced across, watched the display on the recorder count away the seconds. 'I spoke to Angela Massey yesterday,' he said. 'She's every bit as upset as you were pretending to be.'

'Bitch!' Wendy snapped.

'Not really,' Thorne said. 'Just a girl who was in love with your husband. She claims he was in love with her too.'

'He wouldn't know love if it bit him.'

Thorne nodded. 'It must have killed you,' he said. 'Listening to those messages, knowing he was going to leave. Sitting there getting drunker. Angrier...'

'At Christmas,' she shouted. 'Of all the times. What do you imagine that would have done to Jack?'

'What do *you* think you've done to Jack?'

'I didn't plan it,' she said. She was breathing heavily, desperate suddenly. 'He came back and I confronted him. We argued and all of a sudden I had the kitchen knife. I didn't mean to.'

'You stabbed him through the heart and then went back to bed,' Thorne said. 'You left your husband's body for your six-year-old son to find.'

'I'm a good mother,' she said. 'I don't care what you think. I was clearly no great shakes as a wife, but I'm a *damn* good mother...'

◆ ◆ ◆

When Thorne came back into the Incident Room, DS Dave Holland was walking towards him, a broad grin on his face. Singing.

'I saw Mommy killing Santa Claus...'

He saw the look on Thorne's face and stopped.

'Not funny, Dave.'

'Sorry, guv.' Holland held out a large brown envelope. 'We've had a bit of a whip round,' he said. 'For the boy.'

Thorne took it. Said, 'Thanks.'

'Not the best day to find your dad like that.'

Thorne nodded, having revised his opinion somewhat. Yes,

one day was pretty much as good as another to die. But December 25th was a shitty day to lose someone.

◆ ◆ ◆

Jack Fielding was now staying with Alan Fielding's mother and father. Their claim on the child had been thought that little bit stronger than his maternal grandparents, being as it was the child's mother that had killed their son. Thorne sat awkwardly on their sofa. Drinking tea and eating mince pies, while they did their best to act as if their world hadn't fallen apart.

'What's going to happen to her?' Jack's grandmother asked.

'What do you think?' The old man slurped his tea, pulling a face as though he were drinking hemlock. Perhaps he wished he was.

'She's in Holloway,' Thorne said. 'Likely to be there a while, I should have thought. A big murder trial takes a while to put together and, you know... Christmas and everything.'

'Wasn't easy finding a funeral director either,' the old man said. 'Busy with all the suicides or some such.'

Thorne nodded, thinking, *well at least business is booming for somebody.*

They said nothing for a while. Thorne stared at the cards on the mantelpiece. The snowmen and reindeer had been replaced by simple white cards with black borders. *In deepest sympathy.* He glanced at the large, brown envelope on top of the TV.

When Thorne saw the grandmother beam suddenly, he realised that the boy had come into the room. He turned and saw Jack Fielding hovering in the doorway. He smiled, but the boy looked away.

'Come on, Jack,' the grandmother said. 'Come and say hello.'

The boy took a few steps into the room. A large plastic dinosaur hung from his fingers.

'How are you?' Thorne had probably asked stupider questions, but he could not remember when.

'Where's my mum?' the boy asked.

'She's not very well.'

The boy nodded, as though that made perfect sense. 'Is that because of the dead man?' he asked.

Thorne said that it was.

Jack took another step towards him and leaned against the arm of the sofa. He gently put the toy dinosaur into Thorne's lap. 'It wasn't Father Christmas, was it?'

'No,' Thorne said.

'Was it my daddy?'

Thorne heard the old woman sniff, felt his throat constrict a little. But he kept his eyes fixed on the boy.

'It wasn't Father Christmas,' he said.

Thorne glanced across at the boy's grandmother. Saw something around her eyes and in the small nod of her head. He thought it might mean 'thank you', but he could not be sure.

Mark Billingham

Mark Billingham is one of the UK's most acclaimed and popular crime writers. His series of novels featuring DI Tom Thorne has twice won him the Crime Novel of the Year Award and his debut novel, *Sleepyhead* was chosen by the *Sunday Times* as one of the 100 books that had shaped the decade. His latest novel is *Cry Baby.*

A television series based on the Thorne novels starred David Morrissey as Tom Thorne and a series based on *In The Dark* and *Time Of Death* was broadcast on the BBC in 2017.

Mark lives in London with his wife and two children. When he is not living out rock-star fantasies as a member of the Fun Lovin' Crime Writers, he is hard at what is laughably called 'work', writing his next novel. Find him on Twitter @Mark-Billingham or his website: https://www.markbillingham.com. For more books by Mark, go to his Amazon author page: bit.ly/MarkBAmazon.

THE BREADWINNER

Sophie Hannah

I do not like the look of the judge at all. My lawyers have told me so often that it all depends on the judge, and here she is in front of me, this person upon whom it all depends. She has curly grey hair and is wearing a coral-coloured cardigan. She puts down her pen, looks at Jessica and her barrister, then at me and my barrister. There is silence as she makes us wait. I can tell from her expression that she isn't frightened to be as important as she is. I would be; I'd hate to have to make decisions about the lives of total strangers. If someone who knows nothing about me is going to determine my future, I would rather it were someone who feels inadequate to the task. If I'd wanted to be told what to do by an arrogant megalomaniac, I'd have stayed with Jessica.

I've hardly looked at her since the hearing began, but I look now. Her eyes are fixed on the judge. She is the one that Jessica fears, not me, although it's thanks to me that we're all here in the first place. How ironic: even when I have an effect, I appear ineffectual. My soon-to-be-ex-wife still thinks she's more important than I am, even though I'm the Applicant and she's the Respondent—those are our new names. I am applying to the law for justice, but in Jessica's eyes, I am nothing more than a beggar who used to share her super-king-sized bed.

The judge begins to speak. She keeps saying 'Sadly', as if it's part of her job description to regret the end of my marriage. I'm impatient for her to get the preamble over and done with. I try so hard to concentrate on her words that my head fills instead with a blurry panic that I'll miss something. When I push it aside and listen again, she is talking about the details of my life with Jessica: no children together, two children each from previous marriages, Jessica being the breadwinner while I took care of the children and the home.

Did I imagine the contempt in her voice as she said that? If asked, she would probably deny that she thinks the husband ought always to be the breadwinner—most people would. Many of them believe it deep down, however.

I resist the urge to turn to my barrister for reassurance. 'Took care of the children and the home' sounds soft and cuddly and easy. It doesn't imply hard work. I would have felt better if she'd said 'Took responsibility for...' or 'The Applicant did all the domestic labour'.

When I hear the word 'financial', all other thoughts flee from my mind and I listen again. '...taking into account Mr Marshall's lack of income, employment and pension,' the judge is saying. 'Mrs Marshall, you at present have an income of £438,000 a year, as well as assets, including the family home, which are solely in your name. It would seem fair, in recognition of your husband's substantial contribution to your family life for more than fifteen years...'

The rest of the judge's words are hard for me to focus on. Is she on my side? Is she about to find in my favour?

She is. She does. *Thank God.*

Jessica and her barrister are both on their feet, protesting.

'Absolutely not,' says my darling wife. 'I'm not giving him a penny! He was the one who gave up on our marriage, not me. You can lock me up for the rest of my life if you want to—he's getting nothing. Nothing! I don't care how long it takes or how much it costs—I'm going to see to it that he doesn't profit from his disloyalty. He left me on *Christmas Eve*!'

The judge sighs. 'Mrs Marshall, the day of his leaving is irrelevant, as are your feelings. I have told you what is going to happen. As we speak, there are people in custody in this country—mostly men, I have to tell you—because they are unwilling to pay their former partners the amount ordered by the court. If you insist on joining them...'

'You can't do this!' Jessica screams at her.

'I can, Mrs Marshall, and I have,' the judge says wearily. 'Now, if you'll let me finish. The percentage of the respondent's income and assets awarded to the applicant is not intended to imply any moral judgement. No unreasonable behaviour is involved in this break-up, and no third party. You simply no longer wish to live together...'

'*My husband* no longer wishes us to live together,' amends my wife.

'I'm starting to understand why,' said the judge. 'Please let me finish, Mrs Marshall. During your years of marriage, you were the sole breadwinner. Mr Marshall relied entirely on your financial support—'

'Yes, but—'

'Mr Rayner, please instruct your client not to interrupt me again,' says the judge, her voice quietly vicious. I no longer dislike her. In fact, if she'd have me, I would very happily marry her next.

'I intend to break new ground today,' she says, her fingers playing with the large oval-shaped amethyst brooch on her lapel. 'To set a new legal precedent. Mrs Marshall, during the years of your co-habitation with Mr Marshall, you supported him and all four of your respective children financially, is that correct?'

'Yes,' says Jessica bitterly. 'We never got a penny from my ex-husband or his ex-wife.'

'And on the domestic front, Mr Marshall did everything, did he not? You had a very clear demarcation of duties: the traditional one, except with you as the breadwinner and Mr Marshall as the house husband.'

I hate that term. I've always hated it. Maybe I don't want to marry the judge after all. Or indeed anyone—ever again.

'To minimise disruption, I would like to create an arrangement that is as close to the previous status quo as possible,' says the judge. 'Mrs Marshall, my hope is that you will benefit from it as much as Mr Marshall will.'

I don't like the sound of that. Not one bit.

'What?' Jessica snaps. 'Benefit from losing half my income and assets? I don't think so!'

'Mr Marshall did all the cooking and cleaning of the family home during the years you lived together,' the judge says in a gentler voice. 'And, to the extent to which it would be unfair to expect him suddenly to embark upon a lucrative career at the age of fifty-one in order to support himself financially at the level to which he has become accustomed... well, to precisely that same extent it would be equally unfair, Mrs Marshall, if you at the age of forty-nine were to have to learn how to use your cooker. I believe you have an Aga? Awkward things, Agas. Using them is a fine art.'

'What?' I whisper to my barrister. 'Is she joking?'

He says nothing. The skin on his face is pale and patchy.

The judge goes on: 'Mrs Marshall, I assume that, like most breadwinners who have never undertaken any of the domestic labour, you are comprehensively unable to boil an egg, put a duvet cover on a duvet or remember the birthdays of your close relatives. Am I right?'

This can't be happening. I must have fallen into some insane practical joke, or a nightmare. 'Mr Marshall, in return for receiving fifty per cent of Mrs Marshall's income and assets, you will continue to cook all of her meals,' the judge tells me. 'You will also clean her house as often as is necessary to ensure that her home remains as well-maintained as it was when you shared it.'

'Judge, this is unprecedented,' says my barrister. 'It's... With respect, it's utterly absurd.'

'Unprecedented, yes,' says the judge with a smile. 'Absurd? No. Within marriages, people take on roles, as we all know. It makes perfect sense for both parties to continue to look after one another in the exact manner in which they looked after each other while together, to compensate for the fact that both will have fallen severely behind in their ability to be self-sufficient in certain crucial respects.'

My skin has turned to cold jelly. This woman—this *monster* cannot honestly be saying that I must continue to cook and clean for Jessica. She must be a lunatic. My barrister whispers in my ear that we'll appeal, that we'll win.

'I heard that, Mr Henderson,' says the judge. 'Or rather, I lip-read it. I wouldn't be so sure. It has never made sense to me that, after a separation—especially now, in the enlightened age of the blame-free divorce—breadwinners are expected to continue to support their non-earning former spouses as per the unwritten-but-clearly-established terms of the marriage, while the cooking-and-cleaning housewives and househusbands are not expected to do likewise. Surely we can all see how unfair and one-sided that is?'

'But, Judge, the applicant no longer lives with the respondent,' my barrister splutters. 'The practicalities—'

'A fool could sort out the practicalities, Mr Henderson. Mr Marshall still owns the car that Mrs Marshall bought for him, does he not? He can either drop off Mrs Marshall's meals himself, or if he's too busy he can send them in a taxi to her house.'

'Who would pay the cost of the taxi?' asks Jessica's barrister.

The judge considers this for a few seconds before saying, 'The applicant would.'

Jessica is smiling now. Whatever she has to pay me, however substantial a slice of her wealth it might be, I am the one who has been defeated, and she knows it. To have to cook all her meals, clean her house... It will be as if I never left her.

'Don't you agree that this is a fair arrangement, Mr Marshall?' the judge asks me. I would like to gouge out her eyes with a fish knife. I disagree violently—my disagreement is like an allergic reaction inside me that has yet to manifest itself on my person —but I can't think of a single argument with which to challenge the judge. What is the reason? Why am I so definitely right? Why is it so obviously unfair? Why does nothing come to mind?

I feel more inextricably bound to Jessica now than I did on our wedding day.

Sophie Hannah

Sophie Hannah is an internationally bestselling crime fiction writer whose books have sold millions of copies worldwide. Her crime novels have been translated into 49 languages and published in 51 countries. Her psychological thriller *The Carrier* won the Crime Thriller of the Year Award at the 2013 UK National Book Awards. She is the author of four Hercule Poirot mysteries—the first new Poirot mysteries since Agatha Christie's death—*The Monogram Murders*, *Closed Casket*, *The Mystery of Three Quarters*, and *The Killings at Kingfisher Hill*, all of which were national and international bestsellers.

Sophie helped to create a Master's Degree in Crime and Thriller Writing at the University of Cambridge, for which she is the main teacher and Course Director, and is the founder of the Dream Author Coaching Programme for writers. She is an award-winning, bestselling poet, and her poetry is studied at GCSE level across the UK, and she has co-written two murder mystery musicals with composer Annette Armitage: *The Mystery of Mr. E* and *Work Experience*. She has also written a self-help book called *How To Hold a Grudge: From Resentment to Contentment – The Power of Grudges to Transform Your Life*, and hosts the How to Hold a Grudge podcast.

Sophie lives with her husband, children and dog in Cambridge, where she is an Honorary Fellow of Lucy Cavendish College. Find her on Twitter @sophiehannahCB1 or at www.sophiehannah.com. For more books by Sophie, go to her Amazon author page: bit.ly/SophieHAmazon.

BAD GUY

Kate Simants

Guy Collier knows, deep down, that it's too good to be true. Because ever since he started—general assistant, Cooper+Brand estate agency—these bros have been closed-off and hostile, doing nothing but wind him up. But here, in this email, there's a door opening, possibly. Just a crack.

Big Guy
Couple of us going out after Xmas lunch Friday. Coming? 8 at the Crown.
DoubleD

Guy peers up from his desk, over the cubicle. DoubleD's looking at him, eyebrows up: *you in?* And Guy makes out like it's no big deal. He shrugs, sits down, but his heart's going like Stephenson's Rocket. Because, *a night out.* His first night out since Freshers' Week was cut so brutally short. He scrolls through the copy he's working on, considering it.

Thing is, they *are* arseholes. Like, proper dicks. That time Welsh and Hungerford humiliated that girl who thought she was coming in for a proper interview? They made her squeeze herself through increasingly narrow gaps between the door and the frame before loudly dismissing her as too fat to do viewings at their smaller properties. And DoubleD even: here's a man who removed a wheelchair ramp from a flat, claiming *cripples were more hassle than they were worth*. Guy might not be a university student any more but he's not stupid. One little invite doesn't make up for them stealing his packed lunch from the fridge every day for months, or changing his voicemail greeting to sex noises so he nearly got the sack.

His mum says he's better off sticking to his old mates from school. She doesn't know that there *are* no old mates now, not even Ben, DoubleD's brother, Guy's friend since preschool. That's what happens when you make the kind of mistake he made on day four of Freshers' Week, and end up having to leave because you can't stand the blowback. Everyone knows what happened.

He should go. A *night* out with the boys—look at him, calling them his *boys* already, fucking loser—is something he can't afford to turn down.

Even if they are pricks.

The rest of the week jingles past. Payday comes Thursday, as does a little visit from the MD who explains they couldn't stretch the Christmas bonus to him, as a newcomer. Just in case Guy missed the subtext, he adds, *especially as we're doing you a favour in the first place. What with the police interest.* There's a snigger from Hungerford, but it's quietened with a look from DoubleD. Later, Welsh offers Guy a coffee. A tentative blister of hope forms.

Thursday night, after he drags a tree home from the garage and gets the baubles down from the attic, his mum irons his second-favourite shirt for him. She doesn't mention, never has, that his best one is still in an evidence bag somewhere. Buttoning it up in the mirror he opens his mouth wide and silently screams until he's shaking.

And in his head, just audible under the Slade drifting up from the kitchen radio, are the months-old Freshers' Week earworms.

Murmuring low and incessant as tinnitus. Questions he refuses to answer.

Like—*What kind of a bloke* does *that?*

And—*Would it have gone further, if her mate hadn't come in?*

And worst of all—*deep down, did you know she was saying no?*

◆ ◆ ◆

Gone midnight. A club, Chaos or Chronos or something. Music and sweat and lights, the sweet stink of spilled beer and body spray. He stretches his jaw out, blinks hard to make his eyes focus. They're dancing, all of them, him and DoubleD and Welsh and Hungerford. Pumping their fists above their heads, the bass whumphing up through the sticky dancefloor. The song merges into that old Beastie Boys Christmas one. Movement, heat, noise, everyone happy, reckless. There are shots, more lager. DoubleD drags them over to a booth, a girl hanging off either side of him. Guy tries to check the time on his phone but his vision keeps skating out away from him. More shots, except Guy leans back, hands up: he's had enough.

D narrows his eyes, leaning right over the girl wedged between them. 'You out with us or not, mate?'

The booze roils in Guy's gut, making the exhilaration of five minutes ago feel like fear. But here he is, with friends. He doesn't want to sour it, or let it end. So he takes the shot, necks it, grimaces, raises it above his head, victorious.

'That's what I thought, my man!' D shouts. Guy blinks and the girls have gone, but there's a pint in front of him; he blinks again and the pint's almost drunk. A new girl, a redhead, is on D's lap. His hand snakes up onto her breast and she squirms, giggling while she drinks, glossy lips round a straw, fake-nailed fingertips stroking the neck of it. D whispers in her ear and glances at Guy. She follows his eyeline, then her hand is on Guy's crotch. Instinctively he jerks away, and she shrugs.

Another shot, a taxi, freezing rain, a stairwell, someone tripping in the corridor. A flat. A beer he doesn't want but somehow sucks down. A joint passed round, the air greying, stinging his eyes. D's talking in his ear, has been talking a while. The girl's got her hand on Guy's thigh now but he leaves it, his cock impassive.

'You can tell me, man,' D's saying over the music. He lifts a glass to his lips, water. Has he stopped drinking? When? 'Come on,' he insists. 'I won't tell the boys.'

Guy screws up his face. 'What—what we talking about?' he asks. He lets his head drop back, dislodging the girl. He wants to go home.

'The thing with the police.'

Guy's heart drops to his bollocks. 'I don't want to talk about that.'

'Yeah, you do. You were a naughty boy, weren't you?'

Reflexively, Guy closes his eyes, but the snatches of memory flash in the dark of his mind. The police at his door; the interview room. The look on his mum's face.

'It wasn't—I didn't—' he starts, but he has to stop, take a breath. 'It was just kissing. I thought she was into it.'

D eyeballs him, grinning lopsidedly, the implication turning Guy inside out with loathing.

'I heard she was unconscious,' he says.

'It wasn't like that.' It wasn't. No-one believes him, but it wasn't. Guy shakes his head, but the movement makes everything worse.

D leans right in. 'This girl here wants it from me but I'm giving her to you, right?'

Turning, Guy strains focus into his eyes. The redhead's tonguing the bottle, eyes on his. *Enough*, he decides. He tries to say it, *I'm going home,* but he can't get it out. He tries to push himself up, except up isn't where it should be, and something's anchoring him. The edges of what's left of his vision go dark. The music dissolves into a single bellow of continuous noise. He tries to grasp consciousness but it's a train on a track, leaving fast, leaving him behind.

◆ ◆ ◆

He comes to, his phone buzzing furiously against his temple. Belligerent daylight engulfs his brain. He answers, shuts his eyes again, wipes a slick of saliva from his cheek.

It's his mum. 'Oh thank *goodness*,' she says as he opens his eyelids by blinding increments. He takes in the room, neck creaking as he moves. 'Where have you *been*?'

He mumbles that he'll call her back, hangs up, discovers it's gone ten. Where *has* he been? Where is he? A bedroom: male, completely unfamiliar. He hauls himself up from the mattress, his stomach keen to share its caustic load with his oesophagus. His shirt and pants are on, but his jeans are nowhere to be seen. He concentrates on the job of locating them and not on the pain that is geysering everywhere, his head, his stomach, even his skin, his face.

He opens doors. It's a two-bed flat, and he's alone. In the bathroom, a mirror. He flinches at what he sees, leans in closer. *How the hell—*

In his hand, his phone rings again.

'Maaaaate,' DoubleD says. 'You are in some serious shit, my friend.'

It's Saturday. He's supposed to be at work.

'You still at mine?'

It's D's flat, then. Guy says, 'I'll be there in ten,' before remembering he doesn't have a clue where he is. He staggers out of the bathroom, finds a window, pulls the curtain aside, scanning for a landmark.

Except D's saying, 'No, mate. You can't come here,' and Guy realizes he's talking too quietly, like he's trying not to be overheard. 'There's a cop waiting for you.'

Curtain in hand, Guy blinks. 'What?'

'That girl, last night. What the fuck were you thinking? We all heard her saying no, mate. I mean, I know you were pissed but fuuuuck—'

Guy hangs up. He stares at the screen, thinking, no. *No no no no no.* Then he sees it, the little number one on the WhatsApp icon.

Kirsty. He doesn't know a Kirsty.

Except he does, of course. Tapping her thumbnail he sees it's the girl from the club—from the sofa. The redhead. Lips pressed between his teeth, he opens the message. He reads. Runs to the bathroom, wretches hard into the sink.

The phone rings again. Not a number he knows. He lets it buzz, watching the green and red circles, his heart howling. He answers.

'Mr Collier? This is Detective Constable Anderson with the Wiltshire Police. We'd like to have a word with you about an allegation that's been made.'

The room contracts. Guy says, 'Allegation.' It's all he's got.

'It's best we talk to you in person please, Mr Collier. Could you let us know where you are so we can send a car to pick you up?'

He puts his hand to his forehead, his unbuttoned cuff dropping away from his wrist. Revealing—what is *that*? He holds the arm up. Sees the marks.

'Mr Collier? We need an address from you please.'

Scratches. Deep, blood-crusted scratches on his skin. He angles the mirror again. The same on his face. An explanation surfacing in his head as the detective repeats his name, severity deepening his pitch.

These aren't from a fight. This is from someone trying to defend themselves.

Clarity emerges. It's not as if he goes through his options, their various merits, their pitfalls. It's more that he realizes, right then, that Guy Collier is finished. He may have squeaked through after Freshers' Week, when the girl said one thing and he said another. But what if this time he really did... do *that*? And if there were witnesses?

No.

With the certainty, a kind of calm descends. He gives the officer the address of a childhood friend, the first place that comes to mind that is several neighbourhoods away. He finds his jeans, makes a lightning search of the flat for anything valuable and small enough to carry: several pairs of cufflinks, a newish iPad, a slim envelope of twenties stashed at the back of a drawer.

He opens the map on his phone, locates himself, determines a route, and leaves. He won't risk public transport. On the street he rereads the WhatsApp message, then he drops the phone into the first bin he sees.

The whole way there he expects sirens, cars slowing beside him, his name shouted through a loudhailer, but he is unimpeded. When he gets back there's no Clio on the drive, and he remembers, yes, Saturdays his mum goes to Lynn's. So he goes straight in, gets his backpack, essential things. Walking boots, his toughest clothes, things that'll last. He will not think about his mum. He takes the emergency credit card she set up for him, and the strip of photo-booth pictures of the two of them that's been magneted to the fridge since Year 10. Nothing else of hers.

At the front door, he pauses, goes back to the kitchen and finds a pen and notepad. He stands there with the pen an inch from the paper. No words come. He puts the pen down and leaves his childhood home without looking back.

No-one stops him when he goes to the bank and withdraws the maximum for the card, no-one sees him snap it up afterwards and discard it. No-one stops him on the bus to Chippenham, then Bristol, then Plymouth. The greatest risk is using his passport, a last-minute foot passenger ticket to Santander. But then he's on the ship. No-one stops him at all.

On the crossing he tries to sleep, but the same dream comes to him again and again: his mother, weeping, stumbling blindly around the Christmassy house, while a blurry-faced redhead screams the same words through the letterbox until the house is engulfed in flames. The words from her message.

You're going to pay for what you did, you disgusting rapist fuck.

◆ ◆ ◆

He finds work on the outskirts of Santander. Labouring shears the puppy-fat from his belly, fills out his shoulders and darkens his skin. Every night he returns to the van he bought by selling the iPad and the cufflinks. Using a bilingual dictionary and discarded newspapers, he relearns the Spanish he forgot after school. He spends almost nothing, goes nowhere, speaks to no-one.

Months go by. He checks the internet in cafes for reports of his disappearance, demands for his return. Nothing materializes, although he appears on a missing persons site. He will not think about his mother.

He searches online for DoubleD, and Welsh, and Hungerford. They are living their lives. He searches for Kirsty but finds nothing. For a shameful moment before he closes down the browser and heads out once more into the burning sun, he hopes she is dead.

One morning just after dawn, lying in the van at the edge of a patch of sun-scorched scrubland and watching lizards hydrate themselves in the trifling dew, the foreman comes for his documentation. Guy feigns confusion, gets in the van as if to retrieve his papers. He starts the engine, and leaves the foreman shouting in a cloud of dust. He will never return to Santander.

In Córdoba there are places where migrants gather as the night ends. Trucks come, men are chosen for a day's graft. He learns how to be selected, deferential and shirtless, showcasing his brawn. In the evenings he runs, lifts tyres, jumps ropes. The repetition and burn obliterate his memories.

One of the men can get fake IDs, visas. Two years and three months after he left his old life behind, he becomes Guillermo Martinez. In his photograph he is dead-eyed, shaven-headed, easily middle-aged. He is twenty-three years old.

He moves again, favouring cities, anonymity driving his every choice. Valencia, Zaragoza, Seville.

Years pass.

In Madrid, there is a workers' café that does good, cheap paella. He eats there every day until one evening when business is slow the waitress, a freckled, mouse-haired girl, speaks to him gently and touches his arm. Her touch is a transfusion, but when he looks into her face he sees Kirsty, and the girl from Freshers'

Week. *Disgusting rapist fuck.* He snatches his arm away, leaves, does not return. He eats poorly then, from packets and tins. He will not think about his mother.

One winter he finds an abandoned place just outside the city, a half-finished building site with a filthy open culvert flowing slowly along the far edge. He sets up there, builds a table outside, fashions a gazebo from sheeting. Along the culvert grow some wild plants—weeds really. He pulls one up, plants it in some dry earth in a broken bucket. Maybe in the spring it will flower.

There are fireworks over the city a few days before Christmas, and he watches them with a plastic litre bottle of no-name wine. A picture enters his mind unbidden—his mother wrapping presents when he was small, hustling him out of the room, laughing. He reaches for the wine, finds it empty. He takes a bus into the city, wanders into Chueca and selects a bar at random near the plaza. The waitress speaks quickly to him, assuming he is a local. He drinks his beer, takes the *El País* left behind on another table, reads it cover to cover. He stares across the plaza. He has never bought a phone.

As he gets up to leave, someone passing catches his sleeve.

'Hey! Oh my god!' the man says in English. 'Guy, right? What are you doing here?'

Guillermo pulls free. '*Vete*,' he tells him. *Go away.*

'You remember me, man? Ben, from school?'

Ben is drunk. He calls his friends but they are drunk too, moving off to find another bar. He says, 'You know what, your mum rang me. Like, years ago. She rang everyone, trying to find you. You'd been out with my brother, right? What happened?'

Guillermo tells him again that he is not Guy. He insists, really does his best. It's not like he wanted it to go the way it goes. But some people just won't let things lie. So an hour later, Ben is at Guillermo's van drinking anis. His exuberance starts to quiet as Guillermo—Guy again, almost, for one final time—tells him the entire story. All of it, leaving nothing out, safe because he knows how this evening will end.

When he is finished, there is a silence.

Ben clears his throat, and looks around as if suddenly sober, realizing where he is. 'I won't tell anyone,' is how he puts it.

Guillermo sighs. 'I know,' he says.

Another hour and Guillermo has smeared his registration plates with mud, packed the van and left Madrid forever. He leaves nothing behind but the bucket of weeds and Ben, who is face-down in the culvert, weighted with chunks of hardcore to keep him submerged, fly-tipped bin-bags covering him from view.

◆ ◆ ◆

A thousand miles away, Ben's older brother Daniel Dugdale, senior partner at Cooper+Brand estate agency, is slumped at the arse-end of the office Christmas party. Daniel, who no longer answers to DoubleD, drinks rarely these days, but today it called to him.

Paul Hungerford, head of lettings, places a pint on the table. 'You've got to let it go, man,' he tells him, wearily. He's seen this before, sees it every Christmas. He offers some anecdotes but Daniel has become increasingly maudlin, and Paul suspects he will soon start to cry. So Paul hustles him outside, because this is not a conversation he will have among staff.

When they are outside he indulges Daniel as he has done so many times before—raking over the miserable embers of the prank they played on the office junior, a week before Christmas, almost a decade ago.

Kate Simants

Kate is an author of crime fiction. After a decade in the London television industry specialising in undercover filming, Kate moved onto an ancient barge near Bristol to write and bring up her family. Her first novel, *Lock Me In*, was shortlisted for the CWA Debut Dagger, and *A Ruined Girl* won the Bath Novel Award. She has MAs in Creative Writing from Brunel University and UEA. Find her on Twitter @katesboat. For more books by Kate, go to her Amazon author page: bit.ly/KateSAmazon.

AN UNEXPECTED PRESENT

Phoebe Morgan

The fact that Adam died on Christmas Day was, contrary to popular opinion, a good thing. It gave me lots of time to think. It's one of the only days of the year when the street we live on is deathly quiet—pun not intended. Everyone's tucked away inside, with their loved ones. Well, with their families. It isn't always the same thing, I suppose.

I sat with the body for a while, contemplating my options. The room still smelled of pine, and a rather heady mix of sherry and ginger. One of the neighbours had brought us round some nasty candles: 'Christmas-scented'. Still, they were coming in handy now, nicely masking any early whiffs of decay. Possibly not what Margaret at number 59 had intended, but useful nevertheless.

Whilst I thought about what to do, I poured myself a small sherry, using the nice crystal glasses his mother had gifted us last year. I sipped it slowly, like my own mother used to do. It tasted sticky and sweet on my tongue, like rotting fruit.

Intermittently, I glanced at the foot of the stairs. I was lucky this hadn't happened when the children were small; no doubt they'd have bounced down here at the crack of dawn and found

Adam themselves. Now that they were in their early twenties, they'd probably sleep until noon, Christmas Day or no. The lure of Santa didn't have quite the same appeal as it did when they were toddlers, I suppose. To be honest, I was relieved when that whole charade fell apart.

Adam's face was odd; sort of shiny, not dissimilar to the wax currently dripping down the aforementioned scented candle. I studied it, the face that is, trying to force myself to feel something. He was my husband of thirty-five years, after all. Surely I could summon a few tears.

After a couple of minutes I realised my eyes *were* watering, but it was only because the flame from the candle had caught on the pine needles of the Christmas tree, and the unfurling smoke was getting too close to me. I blew the thing out, irritated.

His jaw was slack; that's the part I found the most fascinating. For years I'd watched that jaw; as he masticated his food, clenched it in anger, lifted it to make a point. Quite an aggressive body part, the jaw. Seeing it hanging sloppily towards his neck gave me a small sense of satisfaction.

I got up and went over to the window. The curtains were drawn; thick, heavy drapes that I'd never particularly liked, but I chanced pulling them back. As I'd predicted, the street was empty. A layer of snow dusted the road; it looked untouched. No doubt the hearty ones in the village would be pulling on their wellingtons this afternoon and braving it to the local pub, but I probably had quite a clear few hours until then. It was vital I got my story straight.

My eyes followed a bird as it hopped sadly along the wall outside the Davies' at number 49. Their curtains were drawn, too, but a garish red Santa waved grimly at me from the chimney top. I looked away. My throat was beginning to feel a bit tight.

It was unfortunate that Adam was in such an odd position, sprawled by the fireplace as he was. I suppose I could have said he was sneaking Santa's mince pies, but something inside me told me that wouldn't wash. It would look better if he were propped up nicely, sat calmly on the sofa—and of course, the whole scene would be more appealing were it not for the rapidly spreading scarlet stain on the front of his shirt. I really *had* to do something about that.

The clock in the hallway chimed—it was a great big grandfather one, miserable looking I always thought, like something out of the 1800s. Adam liked it; he said it gave our house a feeling of grandeur. Perhaps I could take it to the skip come the New Year. Or get one of the children to pop it on eBay.

It was ten o'clock in the morning. I was still in my nightie. I had to think of a way of getting Adam out of here, and fast.

Moving quickly, I closed the door to the living room and stuck the 'Do not enter—Santa is busy!' sign up. It had successfully kept the children out of there when they were younger; who was to say it might not work now? Perhaps they'd think it charming.

Upstairs, I pulled on a pair of jeans—not very festive, but endlessly practical—and the jumper I'd been wearing the night before. Now that *was* festive—silver with a sequinned bauble. Another one for eBay.

Adam's woolly hat was resting on the edge of the chair in our bedroom, and I pulled that on too. It was cold outside, judging by the look of that snow. The garage would no doubt be chilly.

Now then, to the task in hand. I knelt down and rummaged underneath the bed. There were five spare M&S rolls of wrapping paper that I hadn't used—they'd originally been for Adam's presents, but once I'd made up my mind I realised that it would be pointless wrapping them up. He wouldn't be able to unwrap them, and Marks and Sparks paper isn't cheap. In a way, I was glad I'd be able to put it to good use. It was just a shame I'd had to go through with buying him a couple of bits, so as not to arouse suspicion—however I'd made sure to keep all the receipts. I'd be taking the lot of it back come January 2nd.

Passing the children's bedrooms, I held my breath. Timothy was snoring, as he usually did, a trait he'd unfortunately inherited from his father. Tilly was quiet as a mouse; possibly still drunk from the night before. I exhaled. They were unlikely to hear a thing.

Back downstairs, the cat, Sooty, rubbed himself against my legs. In all the excitement I'd forgotten to feed him, and that's when the first pang of guilt really hit me. What kind of woman was I, letting the poor creature starve on Christmas of all days? I opened a quick can of Whiskas, trying not to wince at the smell. Sooty mewled gratefully, and we exchanged a little look. His big green eyes blinked up at me. He'd never liked Adam, either, not since my husband had kicked him down the stairs. I sensed approval in the flick of his tail.

I thought I'd better put the oven on, too. The turkey wasn't going to cook itself.

By the time I returned to the living room, I was relieved to see that the blood on Adam's shirt had turned a rusty, dry sort of colour. Either way, it was no longer dripping out onto the carpet. I set about rolling him over, grunting a little as I did so. At least this year he wouldn't be adding to his waistline with another Christmas dinner. He always did eat far too much.

Spreading the wrapping paper out on the floor, I carefully eased him onto it. The pattern was bright; red and green holly leaves, and it clashed terribly with his shirt. Still, that couldn't be helped. It was a job; I'll tell you that. It took me quite a while to wrap it all the way round him, and longer still to go round again and again. One layer simply wouldn't cut it. Even if the roll was a hefty £5.99.

I fetched some ribbon from the drawer in the kitchen; gold, Clintons' finest. It was quite satisfying looping it around the body; I toyed briefly with the idea of curling the ends but decided it was a step too far. I didn't want anyone thinking I'd been frivolous with any of this. It was, after all, quite a serious matter.

I hesitated a bit when I got to his face. Thankfully, his eyes were closed; I don't think I'd have coped well with them gazing up at me as I tried to fit the paper over the awkward shape of his nose. I did another extra layer on the face; with any luck his beak wouldn't poke through and tear the paper.

His feet were easy; he hadn't been wearing shoes, and in fact the sight of his socks disappearing beneath the jaunty paper made me feel quite chipper. I wouldn't be washing any more of *those.*

I was about to step back and admire my handiwork when there was a sound upstairs; the unmistakeable noise of footsteps on the landing. I froze. Perhaps Tilly was going to the bathroom to vomit; she'd clearly had a fair few drinks at the Eight Bells last night with her friends. My breathing felt laboured, and when I touched my brow there was a slight sheen of sweat. What would the children see if they came down now? A large parcel, certainly. I wondered what they'd think it was. A fold-up bicycle, perhaps? A piece of furniture? Both of my offspring had asked for money, this year, and I couldn't very well convince them that it was an unusually shaped pile of £10 notes.

The footsteps upstairs headed in the direction of the bathroom, and I breathed out slowly. There was nothing to worry about. They both thought their father was safely asleep in bed. Presumably they thought the two of us still snuggled up together, cosy as peas in a pod. Children, I find, are relatively easy to deceive.

I left the living room and its contents, and went into the little utility room that leads off from the kitchen. My gloves were lying at the top of the drawer, exactly where I'd put them. I wriggled my hands in, noticing the glint of my wedding ring (eBay?) as I did so, then eased open the back door and examined the wheelbarrow. It was standing next to a pile of logs that we'd had delivered yesterday; nobody wanted to run out over winter. I eyed the barrow critically; it wasn't quite big enough, but it would have to do. If I dragged him across the floor that paper would surely tear, and God knows what might be exposed. No, the only way to do this was to heft him onto the barrow and wheel him quickly through the house to the garage. Then I'd be next to the car; home and dry. I'd already lined the boot with tarpaulin the day before; everybody thought I'd been off peeling the sprouts and no-one had volunteered to help.

Which reminded me. Best get the potatoes on.

To my annoyance the wheelbarrow left a little black trail of grime as I steered it back to the sitting room. It was possible that neither of the kids would notice, but it was the sort of thing the police would pick up like a shot. Of course, my intention was that they never darkened the door, but I couldn't be sure yet.

There was still quite a lot to do first.

Adam's body folded itself into the barrow with a rather gruesome kind of ease. It took all the strength I had to wheel him back through the house, out into the garage, but I breathed a sigh of relief once I got him out of the house itself. Unlocking the car, I smoothed the blue tarpaulin down neatly and then tipped him in; it wasn't graceful by any measure, but it wasn't too bad. I could see my breath misting in front of me, like a tiny white ghost. I closed the lid of the boot with a satisfying clunk and glanced at my watch. It was nearing eleven o'clock. My teachers did always say I was efficient.

I closed the door to the garage and headed back to the scene of the crime. All in all, it wasn't too bad. There was a bit of a stain on the living room carpet, but I didn't think it was anything bleach wouldn't sort out, and in the meantime I thought I'd shift the tree over a metre or so to cover it. The bloody thing dropped hundreds of needles as I did so. I'd deliberately bought one that promised no shedding. Honestly, what had the extra twenty quid been for?

That done, there was the matter of the knife. It sat nonchalantly on the edge of the fireplace, glazed in blood. The sight of it reminded me that I'd have to ask one of the kids to make the cranberry sauce this year; it was usually about the only thing Adam did and obviously this year he'd be indisposed. Timothy would do it, surely. He'd probably be a dab hand.

I picked it up, remembering as I did so the weight of it in my palm a few hours before. I could still feel the strange sensation of it sliding into his flesh; there had been resistance, at first, both from his body and from his mouth as he spluttered at me in disbelief. I'd smiled grimly at him throughout. I could tell he was surprised, but that only made me drive it in just that little bit deeper.

I'd pictured it gliding through his ribcage, puncturing something important—a lung perhaps, or ideally the heart. I imagined them as fleshy balloons, like the children used to play with, and then my unexpected blade popping them like a pin. It was an interesting image; one that stuck in my head.

He'd passed quite quickly, all in all. I was intensely relieved. In life, he'd been loud, aggressive, and yes, violent—but in death he was quiet, and still. Not with a bang, but with a whimper.

I carried the knife into the kitchen, rinsed it under the sink. I really had to start cooking or the children would know something was up. The bottle of sherry was still on the side and I poured another small glass, surprised to see that my fingers were shaking slightly. *Pull yourself together, Charlotte*, I told myself crossly.

I spent quite a happy few hours in the kitchen, getting everything ready, going through the ritual of preparing Christmas lunch. I'd suddenly developed a bit of an appetite, and now that there was nobody around telling me to watch my figure I could eat what I liked. The thought was liberating; I reached for the mince pies. On the radio, Slade was blasting out, and I found myself humming along to the chorus.

That was how Timothy and Tilly found me.

'Merry Christmas, Mum,' Tilly said, putting her arms around me, and I kissed the top of her head.

'Happy Christmas my love. Did you sleep OK?'

She nodded, yawned like a cat.

'Where's Dad?'

I was ready. 'He's popped out my love, a work thing I'm afraid.'

'On Christmas Day?'

I nodded, and focused on the stove. Both of us pretended not to notice the relief on her face. It wasn't only me Adam took his feelings out on. Perhaps kids weren't as easy to deceive as I'd thought.

Timothy was happy to do the cranberry sauce, and in fact it tasted delicious. At around 1pm, I pretended to receive a text from their father, and informed them that he was still tied up at the office. Again, a collective sigh of relief went round the table, and Tilly suggested the two of us pull a cracker.

At 2pm, I lifted the turkey out of the oven, and set it proudly on the table. The candles were burning, the cutlery gleamed; I had to admit the whole thing looked delicious. Like something off a Christmas card.

'Do you want to carve, darling?' I asked Timothy, glancing at my watch. 'It looks like your father's running later than planned.'

'That's ok Mum, you can do it,' my darling boy said, and with that I plunged the knife into the bird and smiled.

It was turning out to be a very good year indeed.

Phoebe Morgan

Phoebe Morgan is the bestselling author of *The Doll House, The Girl Next Door*, and *The Babysitter*. Her books have sold over 150,000 copies, been translated into nine languages and are also available in Canada and the US. She is also an Editorial Director at HarperCollins UK. You can find her on Twitter @Phoebe_A_Morgan, Instagram @phoebeannmorgan and Facebook @PhoebeMorganAuthor. She also blogs about writing and publishing at https://www.phoebemorganauthor.com. For more books by Phoebe, go to her Amazon author page: bit.ly/PhoebeMAmazon.

JUST KIDS

S.R. Masters

It was 1am and the kids were outside again.

The muscles in Frank's neck and abdomen tensed as he lay on his back in the darkness. At first he tried to ignore the noise: bullish half-shouts in newly broken voices, occasionally punctuated by high pitched, girlish laughter. He reached over to the other side of the bed and pulled Sophie closer, being careful not to press too hard against the baby bump; he pushed his exposed ear against her back to block out the sound. But it found a way through all the same.

He gave up trying to sleep and went over to the window. Most of the street was visible through the net curtains but the kids were standing out of sight at the foot of the building three storeys below. To see them, he had to open the window, which he did as quietly as possible.

There were five of them: three boys and two girls. One boy sat on a moped with L plates while the rest sat up against the wall of Frank's building.

Frank considered shouting something, telling them to clear off.

If it were the 1960s he would. Things, teenagers and men, were made differently then. Now, it was different.

Though Frank could not attest directly to the veracity of the claim, having been born in the mid 1980s, those of his father's generation expressed the opinion repeatedly on talk radio.

And it was bad out there.

A lawyer had been stabbed by a gang of fourteen-year-olds at Camden Tube Station recently. That was just three miles away. Some of the kids had never been caught.

There was no guarantee that *these* kids weren't *those* kids.

Shouting would draw attention to himself. They would know where he lived.

He shut the window and another round of laughter rose up from below. Had they seen him?

Frank got back into bed but didn't lie down; instead he sat up against the wall with only his legs beneath the covers. It was so damn cold out there. If that didn't put them off what would?

There was always the police. Perhaps a bit strong to begin with. What about Community Support Officers? He could say he was concerned for the welfare of his elderly neighbour, rather than his own.

'They're just kids' is what Sophie would say, and in the past he would have agreed—back when the kids were only turning up sporadically. But three times in a week was too much. Something needed to be done.

On his way home from work the next day, he braved the Christmas crowds and stopped at the Poundworld near the flat. He found a bag of earplugs at the very back of the shop but another, more colourful bag nearby grabbed his attention.

WATER BALLOON BUMPER FUN PACK

Frank took both bags to the counter.

◆ ◆ ◆

He sat at the dinner table with a beer later that evening. Sophie was opposite him reading a copy of the day's *Metro* that Frank had brought back with him from his commute.

'What did you get?' Sophie asked, looking at the Poundworld bag hanging on the back of Frank's chair.

He searched for a lie, but his pause grew too long. 'Ear plugs and water balloons. I'm going to drop the balloons on those kids if the ear plugs don't work. Or maybe I'll drop them anyway.'

'Oh good. That sounds like a great idea. Let me know how that goes.' She shook her head and looked back down at the paper.

He searched for a witty riposte but again, too much time passed. Instead, he said: 'I will,' and went upstairs to put the bag under their bed.

They came back two days later. Friday night.

It was the engine of the moped that woke him and the shouting that kept him that way.

Why couldn't they just talk? It would be fine if they just talked.

In the mess of voices he could occasionally pick out something meaningful, a swear or a sex word.

Slowly, he rolled onto his stomach and reached under the bed.

Sophie stirred. 'Frank?'

He made his voice sound sleepy. 'Yeah.'

'You okay?'

'Yes. Just rolling over.' His fingers brushed the bag of balloons.

'Don't bother them. They'll be gone in a minute.'

He pulled his hand back reluctantly and rolled over again to hug her. 'I wasn't going to. I just wanted to get my ear plugs.'

He had to wait two weeks to use the balloons.

Sophie's sister asked Sophie to visit her in Cornwall. She had been arguing with her alcoholic boyfriend, and they were on the verge of splitting up for the second time that year.

'You don't mind being on your own?' Sophie asked.

'Not at all. I'll put the tree up while you're gone. Crack out some ready-made eggnog. Have myself a grand old time.'

'Lovely, lonely eggnog. I'm jealous.'

She left on Thursday night and on the way home from work on Friday, Frank stopped to pick up a four pack of Czech beer, which he finished while watching *Lethal Weapon 3*. As he lay in bed at midnight, he heard laughter outside. They were early.

Frank climbed out of bed and opened the window. There were only two of them and they stood against the wall smoking, their mopeds up on kickstands. The kids were directly beneath him.

He listened to their conversation. One of them thought 'Carly' was a slag, while the other thought she was a laugh. They both agreed she was 'F to F' which Frank had a good idea meant the girl was attractive.

Not long after, another helmeted spectre pulled off the road and joined them. This one stayed on his moped and left the sputtering little engine running. Frank waited for them to realise they might be making a bit too much noise, but all that happened was the kid on the bike took off his helmet to make himself at home.

All the better to soak his head.

Frank had seen enough. He retrieved the Poundworld bag from under the bed and with slightly drunken enthusiasm, pulled the seam of the bag. The cheap plastic split too readily. Balloons fell to the floor in all directions. He picked up three and went to the bathroom. The first balloon he filled was red and Frank was pleased with the way the end clung to the tap so that he didn't have to hold it in place. It swelled like fruit filmed by a time-lapse camera.

When all three were full, he carefully navigated his way to the window and peered out again. The three kids were stood in a huddle around the moped belonging to the most recent arrival

—just three feet away from the wall of Frank's building.

It was too perfect. They were right below the window.

With the ends of all three balloons clasped between the four fingers and thumb of his right hand, Frank leaned out of the window as far as he could and tossed the balloons underarm. Then in the same movement, the handle already in his left hand, he pulled the window shut and ducked down beneath the sill.

He waited; nothing happened.

For a long while all Frank could hear was his own excited heart in his ears. Eventually he heard muttering voices, followed shortly after by the pathetic gunning of bike engines.

They were leaving.

Frank stood back up and watched as all three of the bikes drove off the curb and onto the road. They all turned left and vanished out of sight.

Had he won?

He opened the window and looked down. From the marks on the concrete below, it wasn't clear if the balloons had hit their target—but what did it matter? The effect had been the same.

Frank *had* won.

It wasn't until later, with sleep creeping nearby and the alcohol beginning to be processed by his body, that it occurred to him that if the kids really were dangerous, he might have just started something he couldn't finish.

◆ ◆ ◆

The next morning, Frank heard clacking outside. When he opened the window and looked down he saw ten kids all sat up against the wall watching another kid trying to do tricks on a skateboard. Each time the kid fell, the board clattered on the pavement.

In the light, the kids appeared younger.

They might even have been different kids. Frank wasn't sure, but he didn't think it mattered in the general scheme of his war. He promptly filled four balloons and dropped them out of the window. This time he heard a few squeals and shouts which made him smile.

After a late breakfast, Frank went shopping. Their neighbour, Mrs Hardy, was bent over picking something up by the wall where the kids had been earlier.

'Hello, Mrs Hardy,' Frank said. 'Everything okay?'

'Look at this.' She held out the remains of his water balloons on her palm. 'They're everywhere. I don't know what they are but how hard can it be to walk over to the bin?'

'It's these kids. They've been waking me up at night, you know. Have you heard them?'

'I've not *heard* anything,' she said. 'But my hearing's not brilliant these days. It's *this* that bothers me.' She trowelled at the air with her outstretched palm to return his attention to the rubber shrapnel. 'I don't think they're biodegradable, you know.'

With a concerned shake of his head, Frank left Mrs Hardy to contemplate his mess. When he came back an hour later she had been replaced by three boys leaning against the wall to Frank's building. He assumed they were boys, but all of them had the hoods of their sports tops pulled up over their heads so it was hard to tell. One of them dropped his hood and leered at him. Frank looked away quickly.

Did he know?

Not wanting them to see where he lived (just in case), he kept walking past the alley that would have taken him to the entrance to his building. At the bushes that marked the end of the shopping parade, he counted to sixty and walked back to the alley, slipping down it unnoticed.

◆ ◆ ◆

Sophie was due back on Wednesday. He missed her, had bought her flowers on sale at the florists next to Poundworld, but when they spoke on Tuesday evening he encouraged her to stay another night.

'You're being sensible, your sister is being an idiot,' he said to her over the phone. As he spoke he peered out of the bedroom window. 'If his temperature is that high he needs to go to the out-of-hours clinic. You should stay—it sounds like she needs you more than I do.'

'Are you sure?'

'Trust me. I've got everything under control.'

'Really? Is the tree up?'

'Tree is up.'

She waited a moment before saying, 'How are your kids? Did you get to play with your balloons?'

'Everything is under control.'

Only that was a lie. The kids had been back every night since he first threw the balloons. Sometimes there had just been two, at other times there had been more than five. But whatever the arrangement, he realised he couldn't keep throwing balloons. They would become wise to it, if they hadn't already. They would see him. They would spray paint the door or post dog excrement through his letter box. Or worse. He had read in that day's *Metro* that some kid in an Eeyore mask had put a petrol bomb through an old lady's door in Dorset.

And this wasn't Dorset. This was London. They made kids differently here.

He needed a new plan; one that would solve the problem before Sophie came home. His mind kept returning to the kid that leered at him, like he'd known.

After their phone conversation, he drank more Czech beer and mulled on the gently mocking tone in her voice. Had there been something else in there too? Perhaps a little bit of genuine sympathy. Whatever it had been, he didn't like being felt sorry for.

Could he maybe piss in the balloons? They did sort of resemble tiny condoms. He could just attach one to... Or he could boil the kettle, put a bit of hot water in there to make them think it was piss.

Why not just scald them? They wouldn't come back then.

He took the empty beer bottle to the kitchen and put it in a plastic bag with the other empties. They clinked together melodiously.

Frank had an idea. He took the bag of bottles and a hammer from the kitchen drawer into the bedroom, where he wrapped the bottles up in a duvet.

Much later, when the passing cars on the street were down to less than one a minute, he descended from the flat, slunk down the alley and began to sprinkle tiny pieces of glass on the pavement three stories below his bedroom window.

He was eating breakfast when he heard a scream.

What were they doing now?

Frank went to the bedroom window and looked out.

Mrs Hardy was sitting on the pavement below, clutching her left leg. A smear of something dark coloured the concrete beside her.

'Can somebody help me?' The waver in her voice was audible even through the glass. He opened the window to get a better look.

That wasn't balloon water.

'I'm coming down,' he called.

By the time he reached her she had been helped to a nearby bench by a group of concerned passers by. One of them was a man in a suit talking to the emergency services on a mobile phone. Another woman sat on the bench with her arm around Mrs Hardy's shoulder.

'Mrs Hardy, what happened?' Frank said, already knowing the answer.

'It's those begging... those *bloody* kids.' She spat the swear word out as if it had been stuck in her throat for a long time and she was glad to be rid of it. 'Look what they've done.'

She lifted her left foot. A semi-circle of glass, the bottom of a bottle, stuck out of her shoe—the tip of a morbid iceberg.

He had only meant to burst their tyres. Frank felt his blood rushing to his face, trying to give him away.

'Yes—those kids. Something needs to be done,' Frank said.

Mrs Hardy nodded her trembling head.

◆ ◆ ◆

The pavement had been cleared of glass by the time Frank came home from work.

He knocked on Mrs Hardy's door. She answered wearing a dressing gown and a foot bandage. The hospital wanted her back in the morning to change the dressing, but other than that she was fine.

'I have a limp in my right already,' she said. 'Maybe now I'll balance.'

'Are you going to speak to the police?' Frank asked.

'The police? What about?'

'The kids, the ones that left the glass.'

'Oh. No, do you think I should?'

Yes, Frank did think she should. He'd thought so all day. It was the perfect way to end it all, make it a police matter. 'You don't know who you're dealing with these days, Mrs Hardy,' he said. 'But if you told the police they might be able to issue an anti-social behaviour order or something.'

'Surely the police don't need to get involved. I'd prefer to give them a piece of my mind. Maybe *you* can have a word with them? If you see them.'

◆ ◆ ◆

'Trouble is,' he said to Sophie as they lay in bed that night, 'she's from a generation where it was acceptable to clip a kid round the ear if they misbehaved. She'll get her throat cut if she tries that now.'

Sophie sighed. It was threatening to become an argument. He'd jumped on her too quickly with it all, not allowed her to settle back in and share her news with him first. He regretted the bottle of wine he'd drunk before she walked through the door.

'Don't the police need a crime to have been committed?' Her voice was low and soft, the tone almost professional—like a priest listening to a particularly challenging confession. She lay on her back with her eyes closed.

He took back the hand that had been resting on her belly. 'What, like littering? That's a crime, isn't it? Or how about disturbing the peace? If I stood outside someone's window every night making noise at all hours...'

'They're kids. Didn't you ever stay out late and get drunk when you were that age?' But she already knew that answer and the words lost power as the question went along.

'I don't think you understand. It's because you don't read the news; if you read the news you'd know how they—'

'You're right, I am incredibly stupid, Frank. And you know what? All this is making my feeble baby brain hurt. So if you don't mind I think I might go to sleep.'

'I didn't mean you were stupid. I just meant... it's not like when we were kids... Or like it was in the 1960s...'

But it was too late. The cause was lost.

◆ ◆ ◆

After their argument, Frank couldn't sleep. No matter how much he rolled around he couldn't get comfortable. His anger oppressed him from all sides like an inescapably hot summer night.

He wanted to wake her and explain it all again, now that he was starting to sober up. Wanted them to be friends again, for her to tell him how nice the flat looked after the hours he'd spent putting up the decorations. And now that couldn't happen.

They came just after one in the morning. He heard them coming, the rapid putt-putt-putt of their engines getting louder and louder until the noise was right below the window. His chest was tight and grew tighter. The shouting began, two male voices locked in an argument for nearly ten minutes. Frank went to leave the bed but Sophie's hand moved across and she pulled him toward her.

'They'll be gone in a minute,' she said and kissed his neck.

He stroked her head in return and waited for her to sleep. By the time her breathing was at the right, tell-tale pace, the kids were revving their engines.

Were they competing to be the loudest?

At the window he waited. The noise kept coming. His bladder was full and he contemplated emptying it over the kids' heads. But he wasn't an animal. Besides, this had gone beyond practical jokes.

He moved quietly to the kitchen and then to the bathroom. After relieving himself, he went back into the kitchen just as the kettle boiled. Taking great care not to spill a drop on himself—he had filled it beyond the little plastic line marked *max*—Frank took the steaming water to the bedroom and opened the window slowly and quietly. He looked down at the tops of three heads. One kid sat on a moped, one stood to the left of the bike and the other was crouching down by the back wheel. All were in pouring distance.

The kid sitting on the bike roared with laughter at something one of the other two had said.

'Go, go, go,' the crouched kid yelled and the kid on the moped began to rev the engine.

Frank held the kettle out of the window and took aim.

A shrill voice cut through the night. Frank nearly let go.

'Could you shut up please, there's people trying to sleep!' Frank pulled his hand back inside and looked over to his right. Mrs Hardy was leaning out of her window.

The kids all looked up and Frank pulled back out of sight.

'It's one in the flippin' morning. Don't you have homes to go to?' Her voice cracked slightly. It sounded as if it hadn't been raised in quite some time.

Frank waited for the abusive comeback and the swear words

to fly. Instead a rather meek voice said: 'Sorry. We didn't know. His bike's broke and... We were just fixing it.'

'Sorry,' another voice added. 'Merry Christmas.' There was some restrained laughter followed by the sound of a window closing.

Frank watched the three kids come into view from his vantage point a step back from the wall. Their heads were down as they quietly wheeled their mopeds away from the building and out on to the road.

◆ ◆ ◆

He sat watching twenty-four-hour news for a long time. He saw a story about a young father who had been stabbed outside his house for confronting a gang of hooded youths who were sitting on his garden wall. Then he saw it again. And again.

It wasn't until the water had gone cold that Frank realised he was still holding the kettle. Outside it was almost light. When he climbed back into bed Sophie didn't stir. She could sleep through anything.

He put his hand on her bump and slept.

S.R. Masters

S.R. Masters is an internationally published short story writer and novelist. His short fiction has appeared in places such as *The Fiction Desk*, *Shock Totem* and John Joseph Adams and Daniel H. Wilsons' *Press Start to Play* anthology. His debut novel, *The Killer You Know*, was published by Sphere/Little, Brown. Originally from the West Midlands, he now lives in Oxford with his wife and two children. He has never dropped a water balloon on someone from a great height. He can be found on Twitter @srmastersauthor and www.sr-masters.com. For more books by Simon, go to his Amazon author page: bit.ly/SRMAmazon.

ESPECIALLY AT CHRISTMAS

Adam Southward

'White or brown meat?' I asked. 'No, wait. Are we doing crackers first?'

Margot didn't answer, remaining sullen and sulky, her face twisted with ingratitude. She looked so horrid when she was like that. The kids didn't dare speak. Debs hid behind her hair, and little Bobby stared into his lap. His nose still dripped. I'd given up wiping it.

They all waited in silence. I'd gone to a lot of trouble, and their indifference hurt. True, I'd lost my temper, shouted, told them all to *sit the fuck down*, but it was Christmas dinner—a special meal on a special day. It was time to liven up.

I threw a bit of both onto her plate. 'Fine, crackers after,' I said.

Would it have been too much effort to smile, to chat, perhaps sing a carol or two? When I was Bobby's age, my parents would be wasted by now, Mum's cheap bottle of Bucks Fizz empty and Dad's Kestrel cans lining up by the sink. True, Dad had normally hit one of us by this point, but he settled down over lunch. Get some roast turkey inside him and he was as jolly as Santa, so Uncle Nick used to say. Except Uncle Nick stopped coming around when my sister Kat turned thirteen, and we never talked about him again.

Kat left shortly after, to live in Cornwall with a new family. She sent me a postcard when I turned sixteen. It pictured big waves and surfers, blue sky and sunshine. She asked me if I wanted to join her. I wrote back telling her to piss off. She didn't send another.

These grey skies were where I belonged and where my family belonged. I'd lived in this house since I was a child. We didn't leave just because things got a little difficult. I'd told my sister that, and I told Margot that.

Did either of them listen?

I knew Margot didn't like the house. I let that go, put it down to a lack of basic taste—I think Margot grew up in an even crappier part of town than I did, where woodchip wallpaper was a luxury and Constantine vinyl floor tiles were considered garishly posh.

She whined. I refused. I still took her in.

I took a swing of Carling. What would Mum and Dad think of me now? A family of my very own, sat at the same table, the same crockery, the same cutlery—quality never wears out, I don't care who you are—gathered for our festive celebration.

I suppose I could ask them. The thought made me chuckle and I choked on my beer, spitting a few drops across the table. They hit Margot's white shirt. I winced. The look on her face was priceless.

'Sorry,' I said, clearing my throat. 'Sorry, dear.'

◆ ◆ ◆

It was a meet cute. Margot had looked so perfect, gliding across the road with her two children in tow, shopping bags tucked under her arms. She'd been to the local store; essentials—milk and bread, some slightly bruised apples. I'd seen her before, of course, but this time I was so consumed with her beauty I tripped on the curb and fell flat on my face.

'Are you OK?' she'd asked, her voice delicate and earnest, causing my groin to heat up, my heart to race as I pushed myself onto my knees.

Margot introduced herself, dropping her bags to help me. We talked, standing in the street, ignoring the icy breeze. I explained I'd lived in this town my whole life. She said she'd just moved to the small cottage on the corner by the cemetery.

Bobby smiled at me that first time, although Debs reserved hers. It didn't matter. Some things you just know, like when your new family walks into your life.

The early days flew by, but with each one we grew closer. I think I saw her more often than she saw me. She was still surprised when I told her what I had in mind, but I offered the rest of our lives to figure it out. It felt right, I knew she could see it, too.

Debs and Bobby weren't quite so enthused, but when push came to shove, they did as they were told. I promised I'd look after them. I promised I'd prove myself.

They moved in shortly afterwards. This was our first Christmas together.

I hoped it wasn't our last.

A gust of wind hit the window. It was freezing outside; snow was forecast. I could feel the draft from under the kitchen door. The room came back into focus, my eyes struggling with the candlelight.

The others had barely touched their food, heads dipped in submission. Were they still sobbing? I thought I heard a peep out of Debs, but she hid it well. Bobby's sniffling had driven me to distraction, but he was managing to contain it.

I peered over the table, realising it was my fault.

'Sorry,' I said, picking up my knife, licking the gravy off. The consistency was perfect, not too thick. A little salty, but I preferred it that way.

I reached behind Margot and sawed back and forth with the knife. The tinsel got in the way, and I may as well have used a spoon, the edge was so dull. I dropped it back onto my plate and pulled the Stanley knife from my shirt pocket.

'You win,' I said, trying to make it sound light-hearted. I was ready to forgive her, forgive all of them. All they had to do was ask.

But even when I cut and loosened Margot's ropes, her face remained locked in fear, her body frigid. Why was she still scared? I'd said I'd let her go once she stopped complaining about *every little thing*. Christ! If you can't forgive each other on Christmas day, then when?

'There,' I said, before turning to Debs and Bobby. 'Do you two promise to behave, if I cut you free?'

They were keen. Was that a scowl from Margot? No, she wouldn't dare. I reached over again and massaged her wrists—I guess they must have been stiff, tied for so long. I helped her move them forwards until they rested on the table. She still couldn't look at me.

'Look,' I said, starting my peace offering, 'I've told you—'

Margot looked like she was going to say something. 'Huh?' I said. But she held her tongue, as usual, her face saying it all.

I closed my eyes, squeezing them together until they burned, feeling the squelch. I pushed my thumbs into the sockets until the pressure caused a deep shooting pain. I tried to push the reality back inside.

◆ ◆ ◆

The dinner grew cold on the plates. It was a wasted effort, I knew it. The potatoes were soggy and the pigs in blankets were unravelling in front of my eyes, a fitting analogy for this most joyous of days.

I heard it then, a steady thump cutting through the air outside. It grew louder until I could feel the vibrations in the floor and the table. My glass shimmered and the pale liquid trembled.

Was this her doing? I peered at Margot. She faced forward, cowering as the sound was joined by a cacophony of other noises—human and machine, coordinated with the monster overhead, approaching with a menace I could already taste.

I slammed my knife and fork onto the plate, taking a small chip out of the edge. It fell to the tablecloth and I pushed my finger on top of it, feeling it pierce my skin, waiting until the blood was visible on the white cloth before lifting it, pointing it at my precious family.

'This is your fault,' I said, burning inside, eyeing them each in turn, daring any of them to challenge me, to say it didn't matter. 'All you had to do was stay. That's all I asked.'

The thumping slowed, stopped in a crowd of silence, broken by shouting in the garden, on the path, at the rear porch.

The kitchen door crashed open, the frame splintering, scattering fragments as far as the fridge, its gentle hum fading as the cold wind raced across the room. The candles blew out, the comforting heat of the house escaping into the frigid air.

From the darkness they came—four officers, single file, crouched and wary as they entered the kitchen. My kitchen, my house.

Two had tasers, the others brandished night sticks. All four paused, taking a few prolonged moments to stare at me and my family, before their mouths dropped open, like guppies on a deck. The last officer to enter turned and vomited, missing the sink, spraying all over the vinyl floor. The same vinyl floor that covered the concrete that covered my parents, after the time *they'd* tried to leave me.

They'd argued. Said it was time to go. Said they couldn't cope anymore. We disagreed. I told them you don't just leave when things get difficult.

Did either of them listen?

I buried them along with their suitcases, Constantine vinyl floor tiles over the top. It wasn't difficult. And no matter what Margot might think, they weren't posh.

The officer took a breath then vomited again, steadying himself on the worktop before staggering backwards through the doorway into the cold outside.

But that's the great thing about vinyl floors, I thought. It would mop right up.

He was replaced by another officer. Plain clothes, this one. A detective, perhaps. She held her breath, held her nerve, cast her eyes over the whole room before they landed on me.

She nodded to two of the officers. I had no intention of fighting. I knew dinner was over. Christmas was ruined, and there was nothing I could do to change that now. But I didn't offer them anything to eat or drink, or even a cracker. They could go fuck themselves.

They forced my hands behind my back, pulling me upright as the figures in white entered. My new family was manhandled out of their chairs. Little Bobby was first. I watched his face as they untied and lifted him up. Did he ever think of me as his dad? In the short time we'd known one another—since I invited him in and demonstrated why he never needed to leave? If so, he had a funny way of showing it, not even catching my eye when they carried him away.

I turned to Debs. Exactly the same reaction, nothing, not even a thank you as they laid her carefully onto the stretcher.

Margot was last. She complained, as usual, thrashing her arms just as she'd done when I sat her down for dinner. She'd never quite relaxed, never quite got into the festive spirit, despite my best efforts—all of my care and attention wasted.

A length of tinsel snagged on her hand, stretching until it snapped. Ruined. I couldn't use it again next Christmas, although I already had my doubts about that anyway. I had a sense there'd be some hard feelings after this—she would take a lot of persuading.

The female detective was breathing heavily. Perhaps she didn't like the smell of turkey. Her phone rang and she answered it in front of me, making no move to hide her conversation. She watched me while she spoke.

'Three weeks ago,' she said.

Wrong, I thought. I'd met my new family four weeks ago, when I fell over in the street and fell in love. Or did she mean when they moved in with me?

She glanced over at the three of them. I saw her swallow. 'Perhaps two weeks,' she said.

Wrong again, I thought. Ten days. Close.

She hung up, turned to the figures in white.

We watched together. I think time slowed a little, allowing me to savour my last moments with them.

'Goodbye, Bobby,' I said, as they zipped the black body bag over his small head, sealing it at the top.

'See you again, Debs,' I offered, wincing as her long hair caught in the zipper, forcing the officer to wiggle it back and forth before closing the plastic over her face.

'Merry Christmas, Margot,' I said, watching her arms being forced against her sides. She still refused to look at me, staring at the officer instead, letting him zip her up, all the way without flinching. 'Sleep tight,' I added, with a smile.

And then they were gone. All because of one argument. I wanted them to stay; they wanted to leave. But I told them, we don't leave just because of small disagreements.

Especially at Christmas.

Adam Southward

Adam Southward is a philosophy graduate with a professional background in technology, working in both publishing and the public sector. He lives on the south coast of England with his young family. Adam's debut novel, *Trance*, was an Amazon best-seller in 2019, hitting #1 in the UK Kindle charts and #2 in the US. He also contributes to the hugely popular *Afraid of the Light* anthology series—short crime stories with all profits going to charity. His new standalone psychological thriller, *The Stranger Next Door*, will be released in autumn 2021. Find him on Twitter @adamsouthward or on his website adamsouthward.com. For more books by Adam, go to his Amazon author page: bit.ly/AdamSAmazon.

THE BEDMINSTER BIRD BURGLARIES

T.E. Kinsey

Even in the winter, Inspector Sunderland enjoyed the half-hour walk to the Bridewell. He could take the tram, but the walk invigorated him and helped to remind him why he was making the journey in the first place.

In the maze of side streets, he passed the neat little houses of his neighbours—clerks at banks and insurance companies, managers from the railway and the gas company. Some of them nodded a good morning and tipped their hats as they hurried off to work.

Out on the main road he passed shopkeepers pulling down awnings and setting out their wares. He greeted them all and exchanged a few words about the weather or City's prospects in the league. Deliverymen and errand boys knew him, too, and offered a cheery good morning as they went about their work, preparing the city for the day ahead. No matter what dreadful case awaited him when he got to his desk, he always crossed the threshold into the Bristol Police Force's headquarters building with the feeling that the people of the city were worth protecting.

His buoyant mood was punctured by the sight that greeted

him as the door swung shut behind him: the desk officer, Sergeant Tooks. He was a big, burly man, with the ruddy cheeks and bushy beard of a jovial son of the soil—indeed, he was the younger son of a family whose antecedents had been dairy farmers for at least six generations. Sadly, as is so often the case, appearances were deceptive. He may have been descended from a long line of genial farmers, but his own disposition was far from good humoured. For while he looked like a Christmas card illustrator's idea of Father Christmas, his demeanour was that of a man who had lost a shilling and found a farthing. Covered in dung. Protected by angry wasps.

'Good morning, Sergeant,' said the inspector as he turned towards the open double doors that led to the staircase.

The sergeant looked up from his ledger and said, 'Is it, sir? I hadn't noticed.'

'Yes, Tooks,' said the inspector over his shoulder as he mounted the stairs. 'I'm a detective. I'm trained to notice these things.'

'Very good, sir.' Tooks returned briefly to his ledger. 'Oh, Inspector?'

Sunderland stopped and turned.

'Inspector Parsons from B Division sent this over and asked me to give it to you when you came in. He said you like the peculiar ones.'

'Did he now? How very thoughtful of him.' The inspector returned to the desk and read the summary on the front of the manila folder in Tooks's hand. 'Stolen birds?'

'Yes, sir.'

Sunderland took the file. 'Five families in the south of the city have had their Christmas dinner stolen.'

'That's what it says in the file, sir, yes,' said Tooks.

Sunderland frowned. 'The birds were hung in sculleries...' He flicked back through the file. '...in pantries... and one in a shed in the back yard. Reports have been coming in since Saturday morning.'

'That's right, sir, I saw that first gentleman myself.'

‘Here? What was he doing up here? He should have gone to Bedminster.’

‘I believe he said it was on his way to work. I sent the report down to B Division but, as you can see, they sent it straight back.’

‘How very thoughtful of them. So you spoke to Mr... Sutton on Saturday about his stolen goose. He said the bird was taken from his shed.’

‘Ah, yes, sir. That’s right,’ said Tooks with an emphatic nod.

‘What else can you tell me about him?’

‘Let me see, now... As I recall, he was most agitated because someone had broken into his shed and stolen his Christmas dinner. A goose, I believe it was.’

Sunderland tried not to sigh. ‘Did he say anything else? Did he give you any other details?’

The sergeant stroked his beard pensively for a moment. ‘Sutton, you say?’

‘Yes,’ said Sunderland.

‘Of Bedminster?’

‘The very same. What did he say?’

‘He said his goose had been stolen,’ said Tooks, guilelessly.

‘Thank you, Sergeant,’ said Sunderland. ‘I’ll get back to you if I need anything further.’

‘Right you are, sir,’ said Tooks, proudly. ‘Glad to be of service.’

◆ ◆ ◆

Sunderland had far too much work of his own to be chasing around solving B Division’s unwanted cases, but he was in a Christmassy mood and it never did any harm to be owed a favour.

He took the tram out to Bedminster and called on the home of Mr Albert Sutton. The door was opened by a formidable-looking woman in an apron.

‘We don’t want none,’ she said.

He held up his warrant card. ‘I’m not sure I want any, either.

My name is Inspector Sunderland. I'm looking for Mr Sutton.'

'He a'n't done nothin'.'

'He reported a stolen…' Sunderland consulted his notebook. '…goose at the Bridewell on Saturday.'

The woman laughed. 'And they sent a detective? Well I never.'

'It's all part of the service. You're not the only victims and it seems especially mean spirited to steal someone's Christmas dinner, so we're doing our best to find out who's behind it and get your birds back if we can. Can you tell me what happened?'

'Well, Bert came home a little bit late on Friday night. I was gonna give him what for—I had his dinner ready on the dot and it was gettin' cold, see?—but there he is with a great big goose in his arms and I couldn't stay cross with him for long. It had a scar on its back, but other than that it was a lovely lookin' bird. I wanted a turkey this year, but we've got our ma comin', and Auntie Doris. My sister will be here with her husband and their boys. Then there's—'

'So you need a big bird.'

'Big as we could get. I said, "We's gonna 'ave a job gettin' 'e in the oven," I said. But it was just what we needed. It was too big for the larder, and I was worried it wouldn't keep in there anyway, but with it bein' so cold out—i'n't it ever cold? Have you ever known it so cold this time of year? So anyway, I said, "We should hang that in your shed. It'll keep fresh out there. More than that, it won't be in my way and the dog won't be able to get at it." She's a lovely little thing, our Mumpy, but she's a terror for nickin' food. I remember last week she—'

'So Mr Sutton hung the goose in the shed. Was it locked?'

'The shed? Whatever would we lock that for? He a'n't got nothin' in there but a few rusty old tools and a jam jar full of nails. I said to him, I said, "You wants to clean that shed out, Albert Sutton. We could use that space for—"'

'And when did you notice it was gone?'

'Bert went out in the yard first thing Saturday for a smoke. I don't let him smoke in the house—poor little Mumpy don't like it. She's a martyr to her lungs that dog. Been like it since she was a puppy. There was one time when—'

'And he noticed the goose was missing?'

'The shed door was open, so he says. He had a look, and there was the goose, gone.'

'And he didn't notice anything else?'

'He didn't mention nothin'.'

'As a matter of interest, where did he get the bird?'

'Tazewell's—the butcher's on North Street. We put a few pennies into the Christmas Club every week and come Christmas we gets a bird.'

'I see. Well, thank you very much, Mrs Sutton. I've a few more people to speak to, but I'll be in touch as soon as I have any news.'

He bid her good day and set off for the next address on the list.

◆ ◆ ◆

Back at the Bridewell, Sunderland consulted his notes. He had visited four more victims of the Bedminster Bird Burglar and they each had a similar story. The husband had come home proudly bearing the Christmas bird they'd been saving up for, it had been safely stored in a cool place, and the next morning it was gone.

They had all been members of Tazewell's Christmas Club.

He went down to the front desk.

'Afternoon, sir,' said Sergeant Gibble. 'How did you get on in Bedminster?'

'Not too badly, thank you. I thought Tooks was on the desk today.'

'He was on earlies, sir. I took over at two.'

'Good lord, is it gone two already? How time flies. You live in Bedminster, don't you?'

'Man and boy, sir.'

'Do you know Tazewell's on North Street?'

'The butcher's? Knows it well. Old Fred Tazewell's been there for years. His father before him.'

'Trustworthy fellow, this Fred Tazewell?'

'Honest as the day is long, sir.'

'Does he have any staff?'

'There's his wife—she takes the money—and a lad for deliveries. They was never blessed with children of their own, but they always gives one of the local lads a job.'

'The current lad—what's he like?'

'Couldn't say, sir. My wife would know. I could ask her tonight if you likes. Is this about the stolen birds, sir?'

'It is. Are you on lates again tomorrow?'

'I am, sir, yes. Till Friday.'

'I have an idea what might be happening with these birds. Would you mind meeting me at Tazewell's at two? I'll square it with Inspector Miller and you can start your shift closer to home.'

'That would be most agreeable, sir, thank you. Mrs Gibble has been on at me to mend a drippin' tap in the kitchen. It's only a ten-minute job but I never seems to have ten minutes to spare.'

'Splendid. Thank you, Sergeant.'

◆ ◆ ◆

Sergeant Gibble was already waiting for Sunderland as he approached the butcher's shop on North Street a few minutes after two o'clock the next day.

'I'm sorry to have kept you waiting, Sergeant,' he said. 'A cyclist got himself stuck in the tramline.'

'Not to worry, sir. I've only been here a couple of minutes myself. That tap wasn't quite the easy job I'd been expecting.'

'Then it all worked out splendidly. Shall we?'

The inspector opened the shop door and led the way inside.

'Blimey,' said the portly man behind the counter. 'That was quick.' He wiped his hands on his striped apron, tucked his pencil behind his ear, and lifted the hatch in the counter. 'Come through to the back and I'll show you where they got in.'

'I'm not sure we're who you think we are, Mr... Tazewell?' said

Sunderland.

'You're the police,' said the butcher. 'I knows Bill Gibble, don't I, Bill? Old Bill we calls him in the skittles team. I'm impressed you's here so quick, mind. I only sent the lad up the police station a few minutes ago.'

'Ah,' said Sunderland. 'Then I'm afraid we're destined to disappoint you. I'm Inspector Sunderland from A Division at the Bridewell. I'm investigating the theft of some birds you sold for Christmas.'

'I'm sorry, Inspector, I jumped to a whatsaname... a conclusion. I should've known better, mind—I knows Bill don't work round here. We always thought it was strange he don't work at the local nick. "You should work down Bedminster," we says to him.'

'We're glad to have him up at the Bridewell, though.'

'I imagine you are.'

'You know about the thefts, though?'

'Of course. They's my Christmas Club members.'

'Indeed. It's a busy time for a butcher,' said Sunderland. 'You must have trouble keeping up with the orders.'

'Not me. I gets a steady supply. I never runs out. Well, 'cept now, of course.'

'You've run out?'

'Not as such, but I'd like to replace the ones as was stolen. It'll cost me, but I can't let 'em go without cos of some thievin' toe rag. They's been savin' since January.'

Sunderland was having to rethink his hypothesis about the fate of the missing birds.

'We'll get to the bottom of it, don't you worry. In the meantime, though, since we're here, I'd be happy to take a look at your break-in.'

Tazewell led them through to the little office at the rear of the shop where, sure enough, there were the usual signs of a break-in. One of the panes of the half-glazed back door had been smashed, leaving broken glass on the floor. Papers and books were strewn about the small deal table that obviously served as a desk, though without knowing more about the butcher it was impossible for Sunderland to know whether that was its natural state.

'Are you able to tell what's missing, Mr Tazewell? Money? Other valuables?'

'That's the peculiar thing, Inspector. The only thing they took was my Christmas Club order book. Black. About this size.'

He held out his hands to indicate the dimensions of a small notebook.

Sunderland thought for a moment. Suddenly, something occurred to him. 'Who supplies your Christmas poultry?'

'I gets it from a dealer up the meat market. Archie Blackmore—'e knows his poultry and game, that one. His lad Jimmy's our shop boy.'

'What's he like, this Blackmore?'

'How do you mean?'

'Is he an honest fellow?'

Tazewell laughed. 'I a'n't never met an honest fellow, Inspector, and Archie i'n't no exception. Give 'im his due, mind—when 'e 'eard about the thefts, 'e offered to get more birds at a knock-down price. I'll buy 'em and send 'em out again so no one loses out.'

'Except you.'

'Well, it's Christmas, i'n't it?'

'I suppose it is, but there's not many who would be so generous. He operates from the meat market, you say?'

'That's right.'

'Come along, Sergeant, I think we ought to pay this Blackmore a visit.'

The market was closed, but the nightwatchman gave them directions to Blackmore's lock-up in St Philips. By the time they eventually found it, it was dark.

Sunderland hammered on the door with the side of his fist.

'Mr Blackmore?' he called. 'Are you there?'

After a few moments, the door opened a crack to reveal a short, wiry man in a threadbare jacket. He had one hand on the door handle and the other behind his back.

'What do you want?' he said. 'Get out of it afore I belt you one.'

'Mr Blackmore? I'm Inspector Sunderland of the Bristol police, and this is Sergeant Gibble. We'd like to have a word, if we may.'

'You got a warrant?'

'No,' said the inspector. 'But—'

'Then clear off.'

Blackmore slammed the door.

Sunderland ushered Gibble towards him and knocked again. The door opened fractionally once more, and at Sunderland's signal Gibble barged it open.

Blackmore raised the ship's belaying pin he'd been concealing behind his back and made to strike Gibble, but Sunderland grabbed his wrist and twisted it, forcing him to drop the makeshift club.

'You a'n't got no right—'

'Oh, do be quiet, Mr Blackmore, there's a good chap. Sergeant—search the place. We're looking for a small black notebook and a goose with a scar on its back.'

'I'm a legitimate poultry dealer,' whined Blackmore. 'I gots a lot of birds here. It's me trade. They's all legal. I gots receipts.'

Gibble took a lantern from its hook on the wall and began a thorough and systematic search of the storeroom. He returned a few minutes later with a book and a bird with a scar on its back.

'This what you're lookin' for, sir?'

'It is. Arrest this man, please, Sergeant. I'll whistle up some help and you can take him to the Bridewell for me. I've a few things to sort out.'

◆ ◆ ◆

It was nearly nine by the time Sunderland arrived home. He hung his hat and coat in the hall and went through to the front parlour to find his wife, Dollie.

'Sorry I'm late,' he said. 'I had to organise the distribution of some Christmas cheer.'

'Then you're forgiven. I've already eaten, I'm afraid, but there's some dinner in the oven if you're hungry.'

As he ate, he told her the rest of the story of the stolen birds.

'I was sure it was the butcher pulling a fast one,' he said. 'But when we spoke to him and found out that his poultry dealer was offering to sell him more birds on the cheap, I began to wonder. It turns out the poultry dealer's son is the butcher's boy. He gave his dad the names and addresses of a few of the Christmas Club members and when they'd picked up their birds, the dad went round and pinched them back. It was going so well that he decided to break in and take the membership book so he didn't have to rely on his son, then nick a load more.'

'But why?' asked Dollie. 'Why steal everyone's Christmas?'

'He knew old Fred Tazewell wouldn't see his customers go hungry, so he offered to sell the birds back to him.'

'The same ones he sold the first time.'

'Exactly. They were all in his lock-up. So I got a few of the lads from B Division to come up and make sure they went back to their rightful owners.'

'You're a good man, Ollie Sunderland.'

'Anyone would have done the same. Are you at home tomorrow?'

'Yes. I was going to see my mother but she's having a friend round instead. I thought I might make some Christmas decorations. Why?'

'Fred Tazewell is sending us a turkey. I wanted to make sure there was someone here to receive it.'

T.E. Kinsey

Tim Kinsey grew up in London and read history at the University of Bristol. He worked for most of the nineties as a magazine features writer before falling into the glamorous world of the Internet, where he edited content for a very famous entertainment website for quite a few years more. He is the million-copy selling author of the Lady Hardcastle Mysteries, the seventh of which, *The Fatal Flying Affair*, will be published in December 2020. Find him on Twitter @TEKinsey, on Facebook at www.facebook.com/tekinsey, on Instagram @tekinseymysteries, or on his website: www.tekinsey.uk. For more books by Tim, go to his Amazon author page: bit.ly/TEKAmazon.

FRESH MEAT

Elle Croft

The doorbell chimed. Holly flinched, and the warm bundle of fur in her lap protested by digging a single claw into the soft flesh of her thigh.

'Ow! Hey!'

The twitching of his single steel-grey ear was wholly unapologetic.

'It's just Dave,' Holly said, scooping up her companion. 'Come on.'

She lifted his body—pliant and unresisting—over her head, lowering him across her shoulders where he promptly resumed his nap, his head nestled against her neck, paws dangling limply against her chest.

She squinted through the peephole and frowned. The frown remained plastered to her face as she swung the front door open.

'Where's Dave?'

The man in the burgundy fleece raised a single eyebrow.

'Uh... hi?'

'Hi. Where's Dave?'

She recognised that she was being rude. She didn't care.

'He, uh... I guess he's sick today? They don't tell me. I'm just filling in. Hey, cute cat.'

Holly gave the fluff on her shoulder a protective pat. The feline didn't bother responding, and neither did she.

'So, would you like me to bring these in for you?'

'No. I mean, no, thanks. Dave usually lets me unpack them here.'

'Knock yourself out.'

He gestured towards the stack of crates on her doormat, and she reached down to begin collecting her groceries. She picked the bags out of the crates one by one, lining them up neatly in the hallway.

'What's your cat's name?' the driver asked as she transferred the delivery inside.

'Santa Paws.'

He scoffed. 'Good one.'

Holly narrowed her eyes at him. He looked down quickly, studying the invoice in his hands, reading it intently to avoid her scathing gaze.

'No cat food on here? Not your week, Santa Paws.'

'He's not some moggie,' she said, snatching the paper from him. 'I feed him real food, not crappy supermarket stuff.'

'OK, sorry,' he said, holding his hands up in surrender. 'I didn't mean to offend you.'

'It's fine,' she muttered, not meaning it.

'OK. Well. Have a good one.'

She nodded and closed the door, then watched through the peephole as he wheeled his trolley back down the driveway. She felt slightly guilty for being so abrupt, but she didn't like surprises. And besides, he'd mocked Santa Paws, so he didn't deserve her manners.

It wasn't the first time her beloved cat had been the subject of a stranger's derision, or at the very least, the raising of an eyebrow. But he'd been a Christmas present—the only truly generous gesture her ex had ever made—a tiny kitten, red bow around his neck, with the cutest, tufted paws that she'd stared at all day, tears of joy spilling onto her cheeks. She'd used the name as a joke on that magical Christmas Day, almost four years ago now, and it had stuck.

Holly sighed.

'Come on, buddy. Let's get the food packed away, and then I'll give you your dinner.'

At the sound of the D word, Santa Paws became alarmingly alert. He emitted an enthusiastic *meow* and climbed down her body like she was a tree, his claws puncturing her skin on the way down. She didn't protest. He trotted into the kitchen, his tail swishing jauntily, his fluffy knickerbockers making her smile.

Holly dragged the plastic bags onto the kitchen worktop, then began pulling items out and placing them in various piles: frozen, chilled, non-perishable. As she reached for a carton of oat milk, she heard the unmistakable sound of Betty's laugh.

She rolled her eyes, stacking cans and boxes and moving between the pile of dry goods and the pantry cupboard while Santa Paws weaved around her ankles, threatening to trip her.

'Oh, God, *her*,' Betty pealed shrilly. 'Don't worry about her. She's the neighbourhood cat lady.'

Another cackle. Holly leaned towards the kitchen window, which was left open at all times to avoid the smell of cat food and litter overpowering the place. She could see into one of Betty's windows, which offered a view of her kitchen. The delivery driver was inside, sipping a cup of tea, smiling indulgently.

Holly exhaled in disbelief. Of *course* that bitch Betty had got her claws into some fresh meat. Young men were few and far between around their area, but still. This was pretty desperate, even for Betty.

She couldn't see her unwillingly single neighbour, but she could certainly hear her.

'She keeps to herself, mostly. Been here for years, since before I moved in. She used to be married, can you believe it? Her husband was a butcher. Handsome chap. But of course, he got fed up. Who could blame him, with that sourpuss—oh! Sour puss! I didn't even mean to do that—anyway, no one blamed him, poor guy. He just upped and left one day, couple of years ago, and it's been her and the cat since then. She barely leaves the place. I guess she works from home. Something antisocial. IT or something.'

There was a softer voice, male. Holly didn't hear the delivery driver's reply. She didn't need to. Pounding a packet of rice on the kitchen counter, she gritted her teeth.

'That bitch doesn't know anything, does she, Santa Paws?'

He headbutted her calf.

Although Betty's version of events was mean-spirited, and only partly true, she'd been right on a few counts, like Shaun's profession. He was a butcher. And he'd left behind all of his precious butchering equipment, which had been cluttering the kitchen ever since. Knives so sharp Holly had to psych herself up to handle them. Tenderisers. Whetstones. And a gleaming grinder, which Shaun had spent a small fortune on, claiming proudly that it could grind a whole cow, bones and all. She shuddered.

'Good riddance,' she whispered.

She put the last tin of chickpeas in the cupboard, slamming the door, and turned her attention to the pile of chilled food. As soon as she opened the fridge door, Santa Paws let out a loud cry and lifted himself onto his hind legs, batting at her shins with his fluffy white paws.

Holly laughed, her anger dissolving. 'All right. All right! Here, I'll grab your food, just give me a sec.'

But of course, he didn't. He pawed at the air impatiently, meowing loudly and winding a figure of eight around her ankles, his desperation growing. She pulled a Ziploc bag from the fridge, opened it, and tipped the small portion of defrosted mince into a bright red ceramic dish, adorned with a white paw and the cat's name in big black letters. Santa Paws attacked the food as though it might leap right out of his bowl, and Holly continued sorting her groceries, a small smile of satisfaction playing on the corners of her lips.

She turned to the chest freezer beside the fridge and heaved the lid open. She pulled a Ziploc bag from its depths, transferred the next day's cat food to the fridge, and began loading bags of frozen veg and Quorn sausages inside.

'This is a jolly mess,' she muttered to herself, pulling items out and shoving others aside. Then she froze. Her face turned white. She looked behind her, as though the cabinets held answers, then back into the freezer. She rummaged again for a few seconds.

Santa Paws, his dinner devoured, was cleaning himself triumphantly. She leaned down to pat him, absent-mindedly.

'I knew this would happen,' she whispered. 'Just not quite so soon.'

She scratched the space between the cat's ears absently. Then she set her jaw, nodding resolutely.

'Don't worry,' she declared to the ragdoll, despite his distinct lack of concern. He meowed in response. 'I'll think of something.'

◆ ◆ ◆

'Right. Bio,' Holly announced, her face far too close to the glowing screen of her phone. She thought about getting up to fetch her glasses, but they weren't within easy reach, and moving meant disturbing the purring fluffball in her lap.

'It's asking me to sum myself up in a sentence. What do you think, Santa Paws?'

A quick twitch of an ear was her only response.

'I think I might just say "Crazy Cat Lady" and be done with it.'

She laughed at her own joke, a short, sharp bark directed at her phone.

'Maybe I should forget it,' she sighed, carefully stroking the velvety fur above his tiny pink nose. 'It's not like I *need* a man, is it?'

He blinked sleepily, showing a flash of startling blue, then closed his eyes again, purring reassuringly.

'No, you're right,' she said. 'It's important.'

She tapped the 'OK' button without much further thought, then dropped her phone on the sofa beside her and turned on the TV, scrolling through the channels until she stumbled onto

Love, Actually, which was already halfway through. She watched Hugh Grant dancing awkwardly through Downing Street. Her phone buzzed.

Picking it up, she uttered a surprised little 'Oh!' when she realised which app the notification was coming from.

'Hey, Santa Paws, check this out,' she grinned, holding her phone out so the screen faced him. He didn't look up. 'I've got a match.'

She scrolled for a moment.

'Ugh, no. Never mind. He's a carnivore,' Holly moaned, dropping the device in disgust.

At this, the cat let out a small half-meow, half-purr.

'No, it's OK that you're a carnivore, Santa Paws. You're a cat. But trust me, nothing good comes from being with a man who loves meat.'

His ear flicked. The phone buzzed again. She picked it up, tapped, recoiled.

'Oh, God. That is absolutely *not* what I signed up for,' she said, her lips turned down. 'Maybe I really should just forget it. This is not worth the trouble.'

As she swiped across the screen, the phone buzzed in her hand again. Her eyebrows slid up her forehead as she read the message, then tapped through to the sender's profile. She smiled.

This guy, at least, was fully clothed. He wore dark-rimmed glasses and a plain black tee. His hair was cropped short on the sides, but the top of his head was covered with a mop of dark curls. He had a whisper of a moustache, and a nice smile. But that wasn't the best part.

'Santa Paws, get this guy. He's a vegan. *And* he thought my "Crazy Cat Lady" profile was funny. He works in IT as well, another freelancer. And he likes animals. Has a pet snake, which is a bit weird. Probably a bit of a loner, but I suppose I can't really pass judgment on that point.'

Santa Paws purred gently. Holly typed a reply, and soon the messages were flying back and forth. As the kid on the TV sang 'I don't want a lot for Christmas,' Holly beamed.

'A date! Santa Paws, this fellow wants to meet me. What do you think of that?'

She took his ear twitch as a sign of his approval. She started typing.

◆ ◆ ◆

'Dave!' Holly exclaimed at the man standing on her doorstep. 'You're back.'

'Yeah, sorry about last week, Holly. The missus was poorly, so I couldn't make my usual round.'

'Sorry to hear that,' Holly said, meaning it. 'Is she OK now?'

'Right as rain, love, thanks for asking. How are you? And how's the handsome Mister Santa Paws?'

He reached out and gently stroked the living stole that drooped around her neck.

'We're good thanks,' Holly said.

'That's the way. Now, I've got a bit more for you than usual today. Hosting a big Christmas shindig, are you?'

'Something like that,' Holly grimaced, and Dave laughed.

'Let me guess,' he said, handing over a bag filled with bleach and drain cleaner. 'You're hosting the critical rellies. My wife's the same, goes mad with cleaning for weeks before they arrive. They're always too drunk to notice, but that doesn't stop her from scrubbing the place with a toothbrush.'

Holly laughed.

'What can I say? I hate mess.'

'Good on you, love.' He handed the last bag to her, and she stood in the hallway as he scanned her paperwork.

'Well, unless you have to do an emergency order in the meantime, I guess I won't see you till the New Year. So you have a merry Christmas, Holly.'

'You too,' she said brightly, closing the door as he walked back to the truck. She looked at the pile of bags in her hallway and clapped her hands together.

'Right. Let's do this.'

◆ ◆ ◆

Holly jangled with nerves as she prepared for her date with Hugo, the hipster vegan she'd been messaging for the past week. She'd been surprised to find that she enjoyed talking to him. He was intelligent, funny, and loved animals almost as much as she did. He assured her he was a geek with almost no friends, but she struggled to believe that. He'd said the same about her.

She pulled the hem of her dress down. It kept riding up her thick, black tights, but it was too cold to go without them. She remembered now why she hated dresses. And makeup. Leaning in towards the hallway mirror, she checked her lipstick for smudges. She'd already wiped her hand across her face twice since applying it, which meant she'd had to start all over again.

'I won't be long, Santa Paws,' she reached down to stroke his back, and he head butted her ankle. 'I'll be home later. Don't wait up!'

He meowed mournfully, and she almost reconsidered going out at all. Was she being foolish? Was this even safe? Meeting a stranger on the internet was how people dated these days, she understood, but there was so much she didn't know. Perhaps she should just cancel, stay home, watch another festive film, open a bottle of red, give Santa Paws one of the catnip mouse toys she'd bought him for Christmas.

But then he wound around her ankles again and she sighed.

'I know, I know,' she murmured. 'I won't get what I want by staying here. OK, Santa Paws, thanks. I'll see you later.'

She lifted him and kissed his pink nose gently, leaving a bright red streak on his snow-white fur.

◆ ◆ ◆

'I mean, it's not like I don't like cats,' Hugo explained, slurring his words a little. 'They're great. It's just that dogs are... just... better. You know?'

‘Well,’ she said carefully, swirling her glass and staring into the ruby liquid. ‘I suppose we have to agree to disagree on that one.’

She stared at her date, surprised how quickly attraction had turned to disgust. He was handsome, she had to admit, although the balding patch at the back of his head had been an unwelcome surprise. His height, too. He’d greatly exaggerated that on his profile.

Still. She could have lived with those things. The date had been going surprisingly well before the *cat*astrophe, the red wine flowing, the gnocchi mouthwatering, the laughter regular. It was a shame he had to go and ruin it. But it was probably for the best.

‘Are you going to order dessert?’ Hugo asked, his eyes unfocused.

‘I have a better idea,’ she purred, doing her best to appear sultry. Alluring. ‘How about we get out of here?’

She winked, then blushed. She was making an idiot of herself. But Hugo didn’t seem to mind.

‘I was hoping you’d say that,’ he said, his smile morphing into a leer. Her stomach squirmed. She nodded and signalled to the waiter for the bill. She’d make him pay.

◆ ◆ ◆

The cab pulled up, and she peered out the window to make sure that bitch Betty wasn’t curtain-twitching. The neighbourhood was dark though, the residents of the world’s most boring cul-de-sac predictably retired for the night. She’d hated when Shaun had dragged her all the way out there to be closer to the mountain biking trails, like his hobbies were more important than her career, or family. She’d been an idiot back then. That was before he made her choose between, in his words, ‘me, or that stupid, coddled cat’. By then she’d grown to love the peace, the predictability.

Besides, too much had happened in that house, now. She

couldn't move—couldn't risk leaving it in anyone else's hands.

'This is your place?' Hugo slurred. Holly nodded, handing two twenty-pound notes to the driver. She took his hand and pulled him out of the taxi, waving over her shoulder and ushering her stumbling date to the portico, where they'd be safely out of sight.

She opened the door, and Santa Paws came prancing towards them, stopping short when he spotted the intruder.

'You must be Santa Paws,' Hugo said, delighted. He ran, arms outstretched, towards the poor ragdoll, who turned tail and trotted back down the hallway, his disgust for her date matching her own. Holly locked the door behind her and led Hugo into the kitchen. Santa Paws was nowhere to be found. He was probably sulking under her bed. It would take some serious coaxing to get him out again, but she knew just the trick.

'Woah!' Hugo said as he entered the kitchen, his pursuit of the cat now a distant memory. 'Some collection.'

He was staring at the comically large knife set on the kitchen counter.

'Oh,' Holly said. 'That. Yeah, my ex was a butcher.'

Hugo whistled. Stepped towards the row of gleaming handles as Holly's fingers twitched towards the drawer handle.

He didn't see the meat tenderiser as it came down on his skull. He only heard a loud thunk before he dropped to the kitchen tiles, his head shattering the bright red ceramic bowl emblazoned with the strangest—and last—cat name he'd ever heard.

◆ ◆ ◆

'OK,' Holly said, closing the last of the Ziploc bags and dropping it into the freezer. She stared into the frozen depths for a few moments, then clapped her hands. 'I think that's it.'

She shut the lid and looked up, focusing on Santa Paws, who was licking his leg on the kitchen bench across from her. She breathed in, the sharp tang of bleach making her wrinkle her nose. She'd cook a chickpea curry tonight, she decided. Try to overpower the smell.

Santa Paws licked his paw, and as he did so, Holly spotted a speck of blood beside his pink nose. She tutted.

'Look at that mess,' she said, tearing off a piece of kitchen roll and dabbing at the red stain on his snow-white fur. She ran her hand down his cloud-like back, inspecting every inch of him.

'I think that was the last of him,' she said. She picked up the once-again gleaming meat grinder, and put it in a top cupboard. She wouldn't be needing it again for a while. Two years or so, she now knew. She'd plan ahead next time.

'Well,' she said, as she collected her cat and draped him across her shoulders, 'that's your Christmas dinner sorted. Shall we start planning mine?'

Elle Croft

Elle Croft is the author of top 10 Kindle bestseller *The Guilty Wife*, and two other psychological thrillers, *The Other Sister* and *Like Mother, Like Daughter*. When she's not writing, she's either working as a digital marketer or co-hosting the true crime podcast Crime Girl Gang, alongside Victoria Selman and Niki Mackay. Find her on Twitter @elle_croft. For more books by Elle, go to her Amazon author page: bit.ly/ElleCAmazon.

HEAVENLY PEACE

Heather Critchlow

Joseph hates Christmas. While Claire and the children immerse themselves in the festivities, something inside him shuts up shop when the tinsel goes up and doesn't open again until the New Year. He watches them laughing, desperately wishing he could feel their joy.

'Wrap that, Scrooge,' Claire nudges the scissors across the carpet.

There is no bite in her joke and he's grateful—it's not as if he's a misery the rest of the year. She knows why he finds it hard. She makes allowances.

Or she did. As Matty and Sasha grow older and start to bubble over with excitement, he can feel her impatience. She wants to share the experience with him. This is the first year the children both really understand what's happening. His family are in a snow-globe of glittery happiness and he is on the outside looking in.

This year is also his father's turn to come for the holiday. Claire has always insisted that their parents alternate Christmases, though he has tried to tell her it isn't necessary to be so even-handed.

'That wouldn't be fair,' she says. 'And the kids are desperate to see their grandad.'

She feels sorry for his father, he knows. Abandoned by his wife, left to raise his son alone in a time when that wasn't something fathers did. *Poor Bill.*

He collects Poor Bill from the station. After they have back slapped and commented on the weather, they have little to say on the drive home. They have never found their rhythm. As a child he followed on his father's heels—he was taken to work in the van when he wasn't in school, given his own toolbox and presented with sweets from pitying customers—but it was never enough to deserve approval. Joseph concentrates on the icy road, longs for Claire's easy charm to loosen the tension between them.

'I'll get the suitcase,' he says when they pull into the drive. 'You go ahead.'

'If you can manage.' The tone suggests disbelief.

He lingers over the task, watching from afar as Claire opens the door and draws his father into the warmth of their home, as his children scale their grandfather like monkeys.

'Let Grandad get in before you bombard him with questions,' he hears Claire telling Matty.

Everything appears picture perfect, yet Joseph can't sink into any of it. Perhaps this year is harder because Matty is five—the age he was when everything changed. Sometimes he feels the memories are only a breath away: the smell of gingerbread or the twinkling lights on the tree bringing them close to the surface, but then they vanish. He could talk to his father about it. But he can't bring himself to revisit those days.

As he shuts the door and deposits his father's suitcase at the foot of the stairs, he looks through to the lounge, sees Sasha toddling over, holding her favourite picture book. He watches his father lift her onto his lap, kiss the top of her soft head, open the story and fumble for his glasses. A strange feeling of detachment leaches through him; he can barely hear the words or his daughter's giggles. He has an intense desire to pluck her from his father's arms. He pushes it down, alarmed by the strength of the impulse.

◆ ◆ ◆

On Christmas Eve they troop to the early carols outside the local church, a village tradition. A few flakes of snow glaze the scene, and Matty slips a gloved hand into Joseph's, the other into his grandfather's, positioning himself in the middle so they can swing him into the air. He holds tight to his son as they launch him. 'Again!' Matty shouts, 'Again!'

By the time they reach the church he can see his father is out of breath.

'Alright Matt. Let's give Grandad a break, shall we?'

'I'm fine. Don't mollycoddle me, boy.' But he stops and leans on the wall surrounding the churchyard. Joseph feels familiar unease, the colour of his childhood—the short-tempered father whose word is law. When Matty touches his arm, he softens his tone, ruffles the boy's hair. 'Not as young as I was.'

'You alright, Bill?' Claire slips her hand into the crook of his arm, leaving Joseph bringing up the rear with the buggy. 'Did I ever tell you,' he hears, 'that your dad used to be afraid of Father Christmas?'

Matty claps his hands in delight, not hearing the derision.

Irritation pulses through him and he unzips his jacket to let the cold air in, flushed after their walk and the glasses of wine he has consumed to blur the sharpness. His father tells this story every year. Maybe it is true, but listening to his childhood from his father's perspective makes him feel he's lost himself. When Matty bounces back to him, he looks at his son and he tries to smile, to still the anxiety.

They take the children home, Claire baths them and persuades them into bed, freshly washed and wriggling with excitement. Joseph reads their story, making them promise they will try to sleep, pressing his finger to Matty's nose, tucking the sheet in around him.

He can't help but turn to memories of his mother: wedging her hands around his body, bundling him into a duvet-Joey sausage roll. Pressing her finger to his nose like he is doing now to his son. For a second, he can see her flushed face; the tendrils of hair that had escaped her ponytail. *Sleep now. Sleep or Father Christmas won't come.*

He manages to bid the children goodnight, conceal the sadness, the anger that she left him with his father. He'd been discharged from the army by then, but she must have known it wouldn't be easy—the nightmares, the shouting, the drink. The fact that his mother discarded him has shadowed his whole life. Deep down he has always known there must be something fundamentally unlovable about him. Now, looking at his son, a fierce sense of unfairness rises—he was so young.

◆ ◆ ◆

Downstairs, Claire is wrapping the final presents in front of the log burner, the pine scent of the tree enveloping them, stockings hanging empty.

'I'll make some sandwiches in a minute,' he says, sinking onto the sofa, trying to steady himself, unable to relax with the image of his mother's face so fresh in his mind. A memory that was loving, kind. The words that came later dissolved those impressions. *Callous, not cut out for motherhood.* The whispers of his childhood. Neighbours, schoolteachers, busybodies.

His father is reading the newspaper in an armchair in the corner. Oblivious.

'Went back to the woods last week,' he announces over the top of the broadsheet. 'Loggers haven't been that far.'

Just for a moment, a small slice of warmth—the woods were the one place his father did take him when he was younger. Hours spent in their favourite clearing, usually with a petrol station picnic of flat lemonade and dry, curling sandwiches. It wasn't much but it was something.

'That's good,' he tells him. 'Must take Matty and Sasha there sometime.'

'What's Matty getting for Christmas then,' his father asks,

folding the paper.

'He's desperate for a submarine,' Claire says, winking and tapping a large present positioned under the tree.

'Submarine, eh? Fancy. I've got him a red truck, like Joseph wanted when he was that age. Always on about the red truck. Wanted to be like his father. Isn't that right?'

Dad's eyes meet his. No acknowledgement of the insensitivity of the gift.

'I don't know, Dad.' He says, unable to agree. 'Maybe.' He kisses Claire on the head, squeezes her shoulder. 'Time to make the sandwiches.'

He needs to be on his own.

◆ ◆ ◆

The red truck is forever associated with that hollow Christmas day. His stocking, laid on the hearth. A pile of gleaming parcels beneath the tree.

'Morning son.'

Gritty words. His dad sitting on the sofa, already up and showered. His eyes red. The reek of drink on his breath.

'Where's Mummy?'

'She's popped out. You open your presents. She'll be back in a jiffy.'

But he didn't want to open them without her. He had a gift to give her too: a clay impression of his own hand, painted red and green. They would open their presents together and she would put it on the shelf in the hall where she kept all her special things.

He must have opened them at some point though, because he remembers playing with the red truck, feeling sick and sad as his Dad slammed about the kitchen, burning Christmas dinner.

They sat at the table, hours later, dark falling outside. She still hadn't come back. He drenched the meat in gravy and tried to force it past the lump in his throat. There were no crackers, no hats. The clay hand stayed under the tree; pine needles dropping onto the wrapping.

◆ ◆ ◆

They eat the sandwiches, and he tries not to feel too angry about the truck; maybe he shouldn't take it so personally. Dad sits while he and Claire clear the plates, doesn't offer to help. Joseph wishes he would go to bed. He needs a moment to collect himself, some time alone with his wife.

He and Claire tuck presents into the long stockings. They line the bigger gifts under the tree and leave the fairy lights on. Matty made them promise they would. Outside, it's snowing in earnest. The children will get their wish for a white Christmas.

'We can make hoofprints as well, now,' Claire laughs.

She has glitter to scatter outside in the garden to show where the reindeer landed.

'Go and check they're asleep,' she asks. 'Before we start. Just in case.'

His father rises from his chair. 'I'll go up and get my presents for the children.'

'I can get them for you,' Joseph offers, but his father dismisses him with a frown, a slice of his hand. Instead, Joseph is forced to follow him slowly up the stairs, the stale smell of brandy turning his stomach. They don't normally have it in the house.

On the landing they part—his father goes to the guest room and he creeps to the door of the children's room, pushes it open. He knows he should tiptoe back down to Claire, but something in the way Sasha's little arm is thrown back, the way Matty clasps his toy mouse, makes him hover for a moment and breathe them in. His father is banging cupboards in his room so he pushes the door closed behind him and stares at his children asleep in the glow of the nightlight, waiting for a quiet moment to leave. He doesn't want them woken.

Thinking his father has finished his clattering, he turns to go, stretches a hand to the cool metal of the handle, opens the door a crack, just at the moment something falls to the floor in the guest room with a thump. The sound picks him up and throws him back thirty-five years to that other Christmas Eve.

He remembers. He remembers like a veil lifting on a memory that has always been there.

◆ ◆ ◆

He'd tried so hard to sleep when he was five. Lay still in the dark in their bungalow, turned on his side, cocooned against the wall with the bright sound of the television flaring from the other room. But he could hear the rise and fall of their voices. Getting louder. So much louder. He stopped his ears with his fingers until a thump against his wall made his eyes spring open.

It was the sound of Father Christmas falling down the chimney to the hearth. When the shuffling started up, he imagined a round man traipsing from chimney to tree, eating the mince pie that he had left out, drinking from the posh glass he wasn't allowed to touch. Then silence. Silence so deep you would fill it with anything.

He lay there for ages before he tiptoed to the bedroom door, turned the handle down carefully, slowly, the metal cool against his hot palm. He opened the door a tiny crack. Out in the hallway, a dark shape pulling a big red sack. A sack so full of presents it dragged along the ground.

Now he looks out and sees that same shape emerging from the guest room, carrying presents. The only light comes from the hall below, making his father's shadow loom towards him. Joseph's chest seizes; his legs buckle and he grips the door handle tighter. He has always believed his mother took the red rug from their living room—took the rug but left her son. A small strangled sound comes from the back of his throat.

◆ ◆ ◆

He flees to the bathroom, locks the door, pinches the top of his nose and takes long, deep breaths. His heart races and his mind pinwheels. He stays in there a long time.

Eventually he has to face him. Feet of clay as he takes the stairs.

'Claire?'

He can't bring himself to call for his father.

'Out here!'

Her laugh tinkles like sleigh bells and he follows her voice through the living room to the French doors. Cold air pours through them. In the garden, his father is using a spade to make long sleigh marks in the fresh snow. His wife scatters glitter and when she looks up at him her cheeks are ruddy, her eyes bright with Christmas magic.

He takes a breath. She is so beautiful. She loves their children to distraction.

'Matty wants you,' he says. 'He can't sleep.'

She sighs and jogs towards the house, still smiling, squeezes his arm as she passes.

Then it's just the two of them.

'You should be firmer with that boy,' his father says, bringing the spade down so it cracks against the patio. 'You never used to mess around like that. I wouldn't have it.'

'It wasn't Father Christmas I was afraid of, was it, Dad? Not really.'

His voice doesn't sound like his own. He hears the pain through the swirl of snow and a rushing in his ears like wind. His father stills the spade, meets his eyes. He hears it too.

'Why do you keep telling that story? Are you testing me?'

Dad's eyes glitter in the chill. He doesn't move.

Something colder and purer than rage boils over inside Joseph.

'Where is she? Mum?' The spade clatters to the earth.

'Gone. She left us.'

'She didn't leave.'

The shrug ignites Joseph. He roars, lunges and by the time he realises what he has done, his dad is lying in the perfect white, one hand on the spade, the other clutching at his throat. Fat flakes of snow alight on him. He grunts and gasps for air.

'Get up,' Joseph hisses. 'Surely you can take one punch, Dad? One hit after all those blows.'

In the background he hears carols on the television. 'Silent Night' mingles with the snowflakes, the notes fall like drops of crystal.

'He's fast asleep, he must have...' Claire halts on the threshold. 'Joseph, what happened? Did he slip?' She rushes forward, sinks to her knees in the snow, loosens the collar of his father's coat. 'Bill, Bill,' she shouts. 'Oh God, I think he's having a heart attack.'

Poor Bill.

She reaches up, pulls him down beside her.

'Joseph, keep calm, it's okay. Stay with him, I'll call 999.'

Then it is just the two of them again in the white-iced garden. His dad's face is purple and red. He groans, just once and his eyes pop open. He clutches his chest. Joseph moves so that he is over him and finds his gaze.

'Dad?'

The eyes flick to him, the panic, the scrabble for breath. It is making him whole again.

'Dad,' he says. 'Where is she?'

The words fall without echo as the snow deadens the world. *All is calm, all is bright.*

'An accident,' he gasps.

'Where?'

'Believe... me.'

It's almost hard to see him this pathetic.

'Where, Dad? Tell me and I'll help you.' His voice is cold, bargaining.

Calculation and agitation behind those eyes. Another struggle for air. Joseph watches from outside himself as he presses his fingers to his father's throat.

'The forest.'

The words rush out, desperate. Joseph believes them. The only place his father ever took him on a day out. Always that same clearing deep in the woods. It hits him now that those days weren't for him. Simply his father checking no one had found his darkest secret, while her son played in the leaves by her bones.

Claire is in the background, tearfully urging the operator to hurry. The same maternal light that warms her eyes danced in his mother's. His father's eyes widen, then dull; he's running out of breath. Joseph could give mouth to mouth; he could help him breathe. He promised help for the truth. He assumes the position, hesitates.

As the ambulance fights its way through the ice-bound streets and Claire runs down the driveway to intercept it, a great stillness envelops him. Cosseted by the silent snowfall, he sits back on his heels and watches his father, listening to the faint choral music. It doesn't take long. By the time the siren filters through the night, he is gone, leaving truth in his place. *Sleep in heavenly peace.* If not peace, then maybe a path to it. To a place in the woods where a red rug lies buried beneath frozen ground.

Heather Critchlow

Heather spent a decade as a business journalist and editor, before becoming a freelance writer and media consultant. Her work has appeared in *The Times* and *Dow Jones Financial News* as well as a range of specialist titles. Represented by Charlotte Seymour at Andrew Nurnberg Associates, she is working on three literary crime novels. Find her on Twitter @h_critchlow or at www.heathercritchlow.com.

THE SWITCH

James Delargy

The switch is stuck. Okay, it's not really a switch, more like two iron levers, but it's been called the switch since I've been here and it should be working. It always has before. As with all these machines, it gets maintained regularly. Has to be. They do an important job. You know, literally a matter of life or death.

'When was this last checked?' asks Guano, flipping the switch back and forth.

I shake my head and try to ignore the audience watching us from behind the screens. It is tough to do, to blank out the small crowd of people there to watch, some out of curiosity, plenty out of malice. I mean, none of us signed up to be on stage. This isn't Broadway. No pretty faces or pizzazz coming out our keisters.

Not that we don't all have our own lines to deliver. Marks to hit. Faces to pull. I'd call the whole thing a charade but it's much too serious for that.

The tension even has a smell. One that's never been scrubbed away, no matter how many times the room is cleaned from top to bottom. The odour remains. Death, fear and sweat. Ingrained into the walls, etched into the leather straps, into the wood even. Reclaimed from the gallows that were used here previously. Or so the rumour goes.

How many last breaths have been taken between these concrete walls? Eleven during my time but I've only been here for two years. I transferred in to try and make a difference. You see, I don't believe in what they do in here. This eye for an eye shit. But you don't want to hear my story. My story can be told anytime. I'm not the one strapped into the chair fixin' to fry.

Casey Tramaine. You've probably heard of her. Lord knows she's been on TV a lot. Plaguing every second show some nights, dragging my thoughts back to here when I want to leave it behind. Stories, studies, documentaries, recreations and even one woman who believes that her soon-to-be-born infant will be a reincarnation of Casey. Good luck to her if she is. Good luck to both of them, in fact.

You see, Casey Tramaine killed her husband and two young kids. Under three years old, both of them. Just before Christmas. A tragedy. A travesty. Caught her red-handed. Kneeling by their bloody bodies holding the knife. And offering no explanation as to why she did it. Not then and not since. Which makes it fucking catnip for TV folks. There's even a made-for-TV movie in the making I read in the paper this morning, milking the final wave of this scandal. She'll barely be in the ground before she's up on screen. The only life after death I believe in. Ashes to ashes, pixel to pixel.

But for now she is still alive. In front of me. Sitting in the chair, strapped, taped, packed and ready to go. Sitting in absolute silence as me, Guano and Hernandez try to salvage this situation, our half-whispers dwarfed by the sounds filtering through the window of the viewing gallery. Especially the sharp intake of breath when asked if she had any last words. As if they expected the pressure or the finality of the moment to uncork the bottle. But in response to Captain Hernandez's—my boss and the guy in charge of running this whole show—question we got nothing but a gentle shake of the head. No flicker of the eyes, no sentiment expressed at all, not even resignation. And I watched closely. She was an oddball for sure. Almost as if she had bartered the power of speech in return for an ironclad will.

It's not often we have a woman strapped in for the ride. She's my first. Guano's too. Hernandez assisted on one years ago. A straightforward roast and toast according to him. Easier fish to fry. Smaller. Weaker. That Hernandez considers the female of the species to be weaker and the fact that he's well into double figures overseeing executions tells you everything you need to know about him. He's as tough as the leather binding Casey's wrists but even less yielding. A man that emotion is a stranger to. Lacking compunction and compassion in equal measure. The wall that protects us from the shit that is thrown at us from above. And believe me, after this there will be shit thrown.

With Casey being female, Hernandez had been forced to enlist someone new onto the X-Squad, as we are known. To shear the inmate. Usually it's my job, which I don't mind aside from the usual stench of sweat and piss. It's amazing how often the simple process of shaving sets them off. Even the hardened ones. It's the first truly physical step in the procedure, after the chaplain visits and the last meal is gone.

True to her nature, Casey Tramaine's last meal was nothing special, just whatever was on the menu. Fries and erasers. What we call the lumps of processed chicken. Covered in gravy. Hardly the meal I'd want to go out on. Double-bacon stacked cheeseburger if I had to but I don't ever want to have to make that choice. Most pick at the food, or eat half and bring it straight back up. For many the final thing they tasted was not their fried chicken but their own vomit. But not Casey. She had cleaned her plate.

So to comply with our inmate's human rights—before sending two thousand volts through her—Hernandez dragged in Oyanda Hurst from C-Block. A dick move in the extreme. He knew she would hate every second of it. All because she had rejected his advances once. Or so I heard.

I was the one posted on the door, listening from outside to the buzz of the shaver and the tears. Oyanda's solely, apologising all the way through the process. I entered afterwards, the clippers shaking in Oyanda's hand. Casey sat stock still on the metal bench, her glorious, long, blonde hair cascaded around it like threads of a golden silk dress that had disintegrated back into its original parts. Casey never looked at it. As if she had accepted that it had gone. Along with her husband and kids.

At the trial, her defence lawyer had wanted to pursue temporary insanity. But Casey outright refused. She pled guilty and requested the chair rather than the stainless-steel ride. Our slang for lethal injection. Whereas some are born to be third baseman for the Yankees or quarterback for the Titans, I think Casey believes this is her destiny. And maybe it is. The sad thing is that she had to take three other innocent lives with her to fulfil it. But as my mom used to say: Destiny don't care what might be in its path. It's a means to an end after all. Like this job is for me. Not the destiny part. The means to an end. With a wife and three kids to feed, my destiny is inextricably linked to whoever stumps up a paycheck at the end of the month. That happens to be the penitentiary service. I never was any good at sports anyway. The only shooting and scoring I ever did resulted in the five kids I have. Yeah, five. My current wife isn't my first time around the block. Not even the second time around. By the third time I was dizzy and fell in love again. This time it stuck.

There is a clack of steel. Looking up, I see Guano flip the switch back to OFF. I'm glad, for his sake that it didn't work, as Hernandez is still on the phone. I can't make out what he is saying over the murmur of the crowd beyond the glass. The witnesses, the family and the press. This will, of course, go down as a major fuck-up. At least they legally can't report our names. For confidentiality reasons. Though my family will recognise the stock description. Portly, middle-aged with a badly set nose. Guano will be characterised as dark-skinned and Hispanic, despite the fact that his most distinguishable feature is the scar on his neck from a boiling water incident when he was a kid. And Hernandez? Swarthy with stubble. Because I am white they won't mention my colour. As if it is the default setting.

As Guano steps away from the switch I step towards Casey.

I'm in charge of the close-up work, reassuring the inmate, even though she doesn't look flustered. She'd refused a blindfold. And the diaper. Hernandez reckoned it was because she wanted to cause as much offence as possible but I don't think so. I think she doesn't want the indignity of wearing one in her final moments. She doesn't care what is left behind. Like her hair.

'How long until lights out?'

Casey is addressing me, her head twisting as far as the binds allow her. She stares at me without blinking, the warm green of her eyes disarming. Even in the cap and with the electrodes attached to her temples she exudes a sensuousness that is only multiplied by the fact that she doesn't play to it. An inherent sexuality, like a gravity that surrounds her. Dangerous to touch.

I feel on my guard despite us outnumbering her three to one. As if she has all the power. As if she has stolen it from the chair and is ready to strike.

'I'm not sure, miss.'

I suppose 'miss' is the right term. Especially given that she killed her husband. At the trial, every witness testified that the marriage was perfect—a lie I understand all too well after two failed attempts—and that they seemed to be in love. A partnership, jointly taking their kids to playdates and birthdays and all the jumble that fills up a parent's calendar. A jumble that is usually divided up to lessen the pain. But not the Tramaines. By all accounts, they were inseparable.

'It's happening today though? It won't be postponed?'

They are desperate questions delivered entirely without an ounce of pleading in her voice. Only a cold need to know. As if not being executed today would disrupt her plans somehow.

'Are you asking if you will be granted a stay of execution?'

I glance at Guano who is staring at the switch and then back at the windows, his bottom lip curled over his top lip as if he is performing for the audience beyond. Hernandez's ear remains glued to the phone, frustration tightening his jaw.

'Yes. I don't want a stay of execution. This happens today.'

Casey Tramaine blinks just once as she says this. Talking to me. Only to me. As if the rest of the room has disappeared. Just me. And just her. I am her entire world. Or maybe she is mine. Either way I might be the last person she ever speaks to. Which means I must ask the question.

'Why did you kill them?'

Her stare continues, the green of her irises seeming to briefly flash a warning, before her eyes and face settle back into the same blank expression she adopted in the courtroom. The one no one could break. The Casey Tramaine from the stand. The Casey Tramaine from the defendant's table. The murderer Casey Tramaine.

'Why do you want to know?'

The question almost stops my heart. And my brain. Why do I want to know? My thoughts stumble under her stare but out of the morass comes the only answer I can find. Curiosity. Wanting to understand the monster. Out of fear that I might relate to it. That I might be capable of the same savagery.

'I just do. I mean, I have children myself. I can't imagine...'

I can't bring myself to say the words.

'Killing them.' Spoken with alacrity but not enthusiasm. 'Imagine it,' she adds, staring at me.

I don't want to imagine it. But now that the words are out there, it is all I can think about. Benny, Lisa and Austin. Gia and Justine too. My other two. The flashed images are fleeting and blurred at the edges. I see blood. But not much more. No details. No actual wielding of a weapon, thankfully. No blueprint I might find myself obeying. I clench my jaw so tight my fillings hurt. A reminder to stay in charge. Remain aware of her charms and of the lure of infamy. I can't confess to be learned, I can't confess not to have the same simple urge men possess towards attractive women. Ask my former wives. Wandering dick syndrome. Hernandez warned us to be aware. Guano insisted at the time that he wouldn't be susceptible. No one, and especially no pretty blonde mama, has ever had that much of a hold on him. Despite him having a sizeable tattoo of his blonde-haired fiancée's face etched on his upper arm. But Guano is called Guano for the rich and potent shit that spews consistently from his mouth. If something happens he has a previous experience relating to it. Usually where he was the hero, averting a crisis. The innocent party tied up in woe. Woe he had no doubt caused by never shutting up. How much of the brashness is real and how much of it he puts on to distance himself from everything that happens within these walls I have never figured out.

'Have you imagined?' asks Casey, her monotone delivery raising the hairs on my neck.

I ignore her. I look up for help. Like a drowning man I signal with my eyes but Guano is staring through the glass as if posing and Hernandez is studying the open manual in front of him, searching our Bible for an answer. This is not something that has been planned for. Last minute stays of execution, yes. Calls from the electric company warning of possible blackouts and to prep the backup generators, yes. Interventions from the governor, yes. But a complete and seemingly irreparable malfunction? Nothing has prepared us for this. All tests had Coltrane—named after the judge who sent the first to the chair—working perfectly. No hitches. Until now.

'Sometimes thoughts cannot be filtered.' That voice again. Like an earwig, compelling me to look at her. So I do. I find her eyes as if drawn by magnets to them. The green in her eyes seems even more pronounced now, a mixture of the angle, the harsh light and her pale skin contrasting against the darkness of the cap.

Her gaze never wavers. Again I sense that I am all that is connecting her to the world. Her last chance.

'Do you need out?' I ask. 'Of the chair?' I clarify even though I am convinced that even if I offered her absolute freedom, she wouldn't take it.

It is kindness that asks. A kindness that means people think I am a walkover. But I cannot switch off my compassion even if many feel she does not deserve any. The chair is not built for comfort after all, slim padding for the back but none for the butt, just a board to help conduct the current and creates a sheen of sweat which is a plus when you're lighting someone up.

'I want this to end.'

'We're doing all we can, miss.' It feels odd to be reassuring a prisoner that we are doing our best to speed up their passing.

Wanting to be away from Casey, I try to signal Guano to relieve me of guard duty, but he is with Hernandez now, working through the manual and eavesdropping the conversation. Maybe with the warden or the governor by now, both incensed at how this looks, how they will be slaughtered in the press. The authorities incompetent. The vicious murderer earning an unwarranted reprieve.

I am so focussed on a conversation I cannot hear that I almost miss the one I can.

'It wasn't me.' That voice again. Casey. Like a dull thud of a hammer.

I glance at down at her. 'What wasn't?'

'I didn't kill them.'

I pause. There is an echo in her words as if delivered from beyond the grave. As if the switch had worked and I am watching a mirage. She shouldn't be able to speak. The only words left should have been mine. Formally announcing the time of death and confirming that the legal execution of Casey Tramaine had been concluded. Guano drawing the curtains across the viewing windows as I instructed everyone to exit. As if telling the soul of the victim that it was time to depart. It always struck me as odd that I had to tell everyone to leave. As if the audience in the viewing area expected the curtains to open again and some encore to be offered. The prologue to their macabre play.

'But it was my fault.'

Casey again. Her voice filtering through my growing unease.

Of course, I know it was her fault. Her guilty plea had proven that, but has she finally cracked? Is she going to beg for her life? Some do and some don't in here. One final swing at repentance. Much too late.

'What was your fault, Casey?' I ask, my heart beating faster, offering to hear her final confession. Executioner, guard and chaplain all rolled into one.

'I shouldn't have left them with him. Not when he was drinking.'

'Your husband?'

'Yes.'

That her husband was a drinker is news to me. It wasn't mentioned at her trial. Although very few details had been given because of her instantaneous guilty plea.

'What happened, Casey?'

I glance over at the phone. Guano is jabbing his tattooed finger at something in the folder. Maybe the reset procedures. Hernandez is nodding, his face a picture of seriousness. The murmurs continue from behind the glass, outlined complaints, as if the audience feels cheated out of seeing a murderer get their comeuppance.

Right here and now there is only me and Casey Tramaine. And something is not right. I can feel it. Her aura has darkened as if all the weight of the world is on her shoulders. As if she is fading away and I am talking to a ghost.

'He killed them. My babies,' says Casey, containing herself.

'Your husband?'

'We hid it. From everyone.'

'What did you hide, Casey?' I ask but Casey is only concerned with replying to whatever questions are circling her own mind, as if putting her last affairs in order.

'When he was drunk he was a different man. I shouldn't have left them with him. I only wanted to pick up their presents. Personalised bears. In town. Forty minutes. There and back.'

My heart is beating so fast I feel disorientated. I am used to last-minute confessions. But usually they are of guilt not innocence. To clear the decks for whatever lay beyond.

'Why didn't you say anything at your trial?'

'Because I am guilty. I knew what he was capable of. I left them alone with him. I killed them.'

Her face doesn't change expression as she says this, her mind accepting the ultimate punishment for her poor judgment. For the crippling inability of her husband to cope. For his flaws. For his deeds.

'That's not true. Your husband...'

Out of the corner of my eye I catch Guano and Hernandez nod to each other and close the folder. Hernandez hangs up the phone. It means only one thing. The wheels are in motion.

'I found him. With my babies. Crying. I had to.'

'Stand back, Morgan,' says Hernandez to me. Involuntarily I do, the order triggering my ingrained submission to authority.

Guano darts into position by the switch, Hernandez in position by the phone. I am in no-man's land rather than against the wall as I should be.

'To your station, Morgan,' says Hernandez, stricter this time, through gritted teeth, his hand on the phone.

Instead of a call from the governor, the plea for clemency comes from me.

'We can't do this,' I say. I believe her. I believe Casey Tramaine. 'She didn't kill her kids. Her husband did.'

'Stand back, Morgan,' repeats Hernandez, his tone suggesting he is in no mood for further delays.

'You gave me shit about not being taken in,' says Guano. A smile threatens his lips but is held to order. He doesn't want to be known as the grinning executioner.

'Tell them what happened,' I say to Casey, trying to plead her case rather than the other way around.

But Casey doesn't say a word, her eyes fixed straight ahead. Somehow, on the precipice, she looks even more relaxed than before. As if she is glad that the truth has been freed from the confines of her own skull. That the burden of truth has been passed to me.

It is her last gift on this earth.

'Fire up,' calls Hernandez.

Guano nods and pulls the levers down.

A sharp whir rises followed by a bang and a buzz that makes the hairs on my arms and neck stand. In an instant the current passes through Casey Tramaine's body, the electrodes directing two thousand volts of force that will stop her heart.

I step back. I can only watch now. I couldn't save her if I tried. And it would be cruel to try, the chair and the electricity undertaking their duties like I had. Paralysing the respiratory centres. Stopping the muscles pumping the heart. I watch her face finally contort into an emotion. Whether it is a grimace or a smile I cannot tell.

All I know is that Casey Tramaine, the woman who slaughtered her family, is going to meet her kids once again.

James Delargy

James Delargy was born and raised in Ireland but lived in South Africa, Australia and Scotland, before ending up in semi-rural England where he now lives. His debut thriller, *55*, was published in 2019 by Simon & Schuster and sold to twenty-two territories. His next standalone thriller, *Vanished*, will be published in April 2021 by Simon & Schuster. Find him on Twitter @JDelargyAuthor. For more books by James, go to his Amazon author page: bit.ly/JamesDAmazon.

SECRET SANTA

Jo Furniss

2020

Mallory slips on her face mask even though she isn't sure she'll go through with it. Her friends are in the pub, in the snug beneath the stained-glass window. Two-dimensional shamrocks cast a pall that makes the women look waxy. Not the kind of light Mallory would risk being papped in. She tugs at her Santa hat and tucks her distinctive red curls beneath its fake-fur trim.

Four women at the table, two speaking simultaneously and the other two laughing. They don't care what they look like to outsiders; they're here for one another, for themselves. Their gatherings have the urgency of an emergency Cobra meeting.

They don't notice Mallory.

She takes a box from her bag and frees the device from its protection, careful with the cables. Recalling memorised instructions, she waits until its lights come on and sets the countdown timer. She holds the device flat on her hand while she looks into the pub.

A Secret Santa stocking is the centrepiece of their table in the snug. It contains no surprises. Not yet.

Jane always gives beauty products, her twin sister Emma a self-help book. Both of them, inanely optimistic. Tatum's present will be home-made jewellery. And Jilly... it's hard to predict Jilly's, but it will be silk or branded or otherwise designed to ensure that the group knows it cost more than the £15 spending limit.

Inside, Jilly gives an instruction to Tatum who taps a message on her phone. Outside, Mallory's mobile pings. She pulls it from her pocket with her free hand. *Everything ok? We might have to order!*

Mallory stows her phone. The women wait four minutes—she watches the whirring clock on the primed device—and then they go to the bar with menus in their hands.

They leave the stocking. Mallory enters the pub, device balanced on her palm. She checks the timer again and works it gingerly to the bottom of the stocking. It mustn't go off too soon or —worse—not at all.

Her stomach hollows, but in forty-six minutes it won't matter. Mallory trots out of the pub towards a taxi rank. On the way, she drops the Santa hat into a bin. Her red hair billows and she hears a fan shout in disbelief: *Mallory, it's Mallory!*

1999

I Have A Dream

And the UK's Christmas Number One is... The voice on the radio is as cheesy as Wotsits, but we don't hear the song over the twins' screaming. Jane and Emma saw Westlife this summer and have been obsessed ever since.

Tatum sings in falsetto until I elbow her. *Don't ruin their fun.* Tatum and I prefer Eminem. My aunt got me a copy of his new album that isn't out until next year. The twins giggled at the swearing.

As Westlife finishes, we knock down the volume and that's when we hear the doorbell. Jane and Emma run to answer: 'We invited Jilly!'

'How come?' I ask.

Tatum shrugs. 'Come on, Mallory. She's new. They're being nice.'

Nice isn't the point. It wasn't *nice* when they refused to let Christopher come to Secret Santa any more. Secret Santa has been us five since forever. Then, all of a sudden, it became 'girls only'. And I had to tell Christopher.

The twins let Jilly have the beanbag. She's brought a quilted stocking with *Secret Santa* embroidered on it. Her mother made it for her last group of friends.

'Was it all girls?' I ask. 'Your last group?'

'I'm not joining a group with *boys*,' she shrugs.

'Why—?' I try.

Jilly is louder: 'Can't believe it's a new millennium!'

'What if the world stops?' Tatum says. 'This computer bug?'

'It won't—' I try.

'The government is using the bug to control us,' Jilly says. 'True, untrue, whatever.' The twins and Tatum await her next word. But Jilly looks at me when she speaks. 'It's necessary to keep people in their place.'

◆ ◆ ◆

2017

Mallory stops dead on the pavement. She hears Jilly's voice in her head as clear as day: *It's necessary to keep people in their place.* There she is now, in the pub.

A group of pissed-up lads nearly run into Mallory, and one clocks her hair, her profile, her figure. 'Oi, you that girl off that show?' Mallory does what she always does to avoid trouble; laughs along.

Then she turns back to the pub where four women sit beneath a stained-glass window. After thirteen years, they still come here! She rises on her tiptoes. They're doing Secret Santa. The stocking is on the table, the same old stocking.

Maybe it's the aggressive twinkling of the fairy lights or the negroni she had before supper, but Mallory's vision blurs at the edges. It's unreal. This pub, this coincidence. It's...

It's necessary to keep people in their place.

Mallory steps back, forcing a woman with tinsel around her head into the road. 'You blind or stupid?' the woman says. Mallory puffs out a laugh. The woman's right; she has been blind *and* stupid. She takes one last look at the four friends and walks on.

Her awakening started with that Secret Santa stocking.

Truth, untruth, whatever.

The events back then scripted a story that has played on repeat inside her head for thirteen years. But now Mallory is writing a new script; a real one, for TV. And this is its truth. Her story starts with Secret Santa.

2000

Can We Fix It?

I turn off the radio before we're subjected to the Christmas Number One.

'What is the world coming to?' I say.

'A Christmas song *should be* about community and togetherness,' Jilly corrects me.

'Yes! We!' says Emma.

'Can!' chants Jane.

'You see,' Jilly says. 'Some people thrive on friendship.'

I put the stereo on the shelf. Tatum flicks through Jilly's CDs and holds one up. Jilly nods and clicks her fingers at me, indicating that I should take the disc.

'Stick can do it,' Jilly says. 'She put the stereo right up there where we can't reach it. She always wants to be in charge of the music.'

It's not true, but I don't want to argue, not during Secret Santa.

'Can Stick fix it?' sings Jane.

'Yes, she can!' calls Emma.

The 'Stick' thing has stuck. The piano intro to S Club 7 starts.

They jump up to dance and I go to the loo.

I hear them through the wall, distant and muffled. *Reach for the stars!* I can reach the door lintel now. I shot up this year. I'm taller than Christopher, who is the only one who doesn't mention it every second of every day. The only one who doesn't call me Stick. When I go back to the bedroom, Jilly holds out the stocking.

'You first,' she says. I put my hand inside. A cold stick feels like —

'A carrot!' I say as it lands in my lap. 'Carrot because I'm ginger. Stick because I'm tall. Funny.' *Comedy genius.*

'Oh God,' says Jilly with a slow eye roll. 'As if she doesn't know she's completely gorgeous!'

'Tall and—' says Jane.

'—Skinny!' Emma says.

'Honestly, Mallory,' Jilly says. 'If there's anything worse than being best friends with a tall, skinny bitch, it's being friends with a tall, skinny bitch who's always begging for compliments.'

The others pick a present, I eat my carrot.

◆ ◆ ◆

2018

Four women sit in the snug, Secret Santa stocking before them. Mallory approaches, the twins grin, Tatum waves and, finally, Jilly looks up.

'What a coincidence that I bumped into Mallory,' says Tatum. 'At the tube stop right by my house.' Tatum had recognised her old friend at once, which is no surprise given that you can't turn on the TV these days without seeing Mallory's face. 'Isn't it amazing?' Tatum speaks too fast, waves her hands too much. 'And you're an actress!'

'Lucky I was good at something, given that I had to leave school without my A-Levels.' Mallory grimaces. 'I'd rather be a writer, though. I'm working on a script, researching it as we speak.'

'It's so good to see you,' says Tatum. 'We forgive you for missing fourteen Secret Santas!'

'Fifteen,' says Mallory.

'Hmm,' muses Jilly, as though the matter is up for discussion. 'We left school in 2003—'

'I didn't go to Secret Santa that year.'

'You left so suddenly,' Jane says.

'We never did know why—?' says Emma.

'I bought a present for the stocking!' Mallory offers a small parcel. 'Don't worry, it's not a Samaritans keyring or anything!'

'Why would it be—?' Jilly's frown concertinas her top lip so that her teeth show. She's *so* bewildered by the suggestion. The twins and Tatum sip their vino.

Ah, Mallory thinks. So we don't remember. *Truth, untruth, whatever.*

2001

Somethin' Stupid

The twins perform an ironic dance that is only slightly less cynical than the Christmas Number One.

'Do you think they've...?' Jane says.

'Robbie and Nicole?' says Emma.

'She's like a foot taller than him,' says Jilly.

'I don't think she is—' I try.

'He stands on a box.' Jilly interrupts. 'Men *hate* being shorter than women. It emasculates them and—'

I interrupt back: 'My aunt works with Robbie—'

'Talk-ing!' Jilly uses a sing-song voice that indicates she is very patient. 'As I was saying, men don't appreciate tall, *dominant*,' here she looks significantly at me, 'women. Anyway, we've got to be quick because of the boys' party—'

The other girls whoop and Jilly allows herself a smile. 'I'm going to push on with Secret Santa. To speed it up, I've done it differently. That's why I asked for your presents early.'

She puts a giant parcel in the middle and grabs the radio.

'What's this, pass the parcel?' I scoff.

'That's exactly what it is,' says Jilly. She turns up the volume. We shuffle into a tight circle, pass the parcel with great ceremony, then loosen up and start enjoying it. The music stops. The parcel is in my hands. Despite myself, I glance at Jilly to check that she meant for me to win. Her level gaze says nothing. I unwrap the top layer of paper. Yellow leaflets cascade onto my lap. Samaritans flyers. I pick one up. *Things getting you down? Are you lonely? Ever thought of ending it?*

The room is too quiet without music.

'Just a joke,' says Jilly. 'Your real present is there.'

I keep my gaze down and blink rapidly while I open a box containing earrings.

'Thank you, Tatum,' I say, recognising her handiwork.

'Wear them tonight,' she says. 'Christopher's going.'

Music slams into the silence.

'Mallory looks a bit like Nicole Kidman.' Tatum looks for confirmation from the twins, who glance between Jilly and me.

'Just pass the parcel, Stick,' says Jilly.

2019

'Has anyone got the first clue what the Christmas Number One is?' Jane says.

'We always used to listen to the Top 40 before Secret Santa,' says Emma.

'When did we lose touch?' Tatum sighs.

'Unfortunately, my kids keep singing it,' says Jilly. '*I Love Sausage Rolls.* Seriously...'

'I remember you saying—' I can't resist '—that songs about togetherness make perfect Christmas Number Ones. Doesn't your family come together over sausage rolls?'

Jilly takes a slug of wine, chokes, and Tatum pours her some water. We're in the snug, in the queasy light of the stained-glass window.

'How *are* things at home?' Jane says.

'With Kit?' says Emma.

'Wouldn't know,' Jilly croaks, 'he's never there.' She sips water and shakes her head. Can't speak. Still choking.

'How's work, Tatum?' I ask.

'Boring. I want to know about your TV show. What's it called, when's it on?'

'It's called Secret Santa, believe it or not. It'll be on Netflix this time next year. It's taken forever to get it made, but finally…' I raise my glass. 'I think 2020 is going to change all our lives!'

2002

Sound of the Underground

The twins have had one glass of Pernod and they're pretending to be drunk. They perform a dance that involves jerking their hips and pouting at a pretend camera.

'Something funny inside—' Jane sings.

'—my mind!' sings Emma.

Jilly pours Tatum a Pernod and adds water. The glass turns milky. They down their drinks while holding their noses. I ignore my glass.

'Best you stay sober,' Jilly says. 'As you can't be trusted.'

The twins turn off the radio.

'What do you mean by that?' I say.

'You know,' says Jilly.

'Why don't you tell me?' I say.

'Why don't I tell everyone?' Jilly throws her hair back. She's had chunky highlights and likes tossing them about.

'You and Kit,' Jilly says.

'Kit? You mean Christopher?' I look to the others but they say nothing.

'He prefers Kit,' Jilly says. 'You have to accept that things change.'

He hates it. He told me. But whatever. Jilly and Kit have been together since their families took a joint holiday in the summer. He didn't want to go, but his mum made him. I think the same might be true about him and Jilly. But I can't say for sure; these days, I only see him at the bus stop.

Jilly pushes a piece of paper at me. 'I took this picture on my phone,' she says. 'Downloaded it and printed it out.' The photo is blurry, printed on regular paper. The ink has bled.

It shows me and Christopher—Kit, whatever—standing close together. It looks like I'm trying to kiss him and he is leaning way back to avoid me. I was telling him about a party I went to with my aunt where this old film director guy lunged at me. I must have acted it out on Kit. Jilly—the mad, stalking *freak*—photographed us.

'Going after your best friend's boyfriend, Mallory.' Jilly shakes her head.

The fairy lights judder.

'I didn't—'

'Please!' says Jilly. She reaches into the stocking. Pulls out a small white box and hands it to me. I open it and there is a single cupcake. She says, 'It's a shit cake.'

'What?'

'I baked it. I found a dried-up turd in the garden and sprinkled it into the batter. If you didn't try to get off with Kit, prove it.'

The twins are chewing their nails. Tatum has her arms folded. She averts her eyes.

They want me to eat shit. So I eat shit. Jilly laughs when I gag. 'There's no dog turd in it,' she says. 'It's just cake. We believe you, Mallory.'

2020

'Such a strange year,' Jane says.

'Horrible,' says Emma.

'Drink to that.' Tatum raises her glass and Emma squeezes her arm because she got laid off. Tatum nods her thanks.

'I've enjoyed it,' says Jilly, twisting her wine glass on its coaster. 'Kids in the bosom of the home, Kit where I can keep an eye on him, just us and the dogs. It's a reminder of what I have to be grateful for.'

'Good for you,' says Tatum and swigs her red.

The twins start talking about the TV show that Mallory wrote, produced and stars in, which is being trailed heavily on Netflix.

'Secret—' Jane says.

'—Santa!' says Emma. 'We're going to binge it when it comes out tomorrow.'

Tatum leans forward. 'Do you think it's autobiograph—'

'Talking of the star turn, how late is she *this time*?' says Jilly. Tatum picks up her phone and taps a message. When they get no reply, Jilly says they have to order. They return from the bar six minutes later. Forty minutes after that, the device inside the stocking goes off.

It happens in slow motion. Jane and Emma grab each other's hands. Tatum recoils from the initial blast. Only Jilly keeps her cool when the stocking emits a honking blare and strobe lights.

'It that one of your presents?' she says.

'Mine's soap,' says Jane.

'Book,' says Emma.

Tatum shakes her head so hard her earrings clatter.

Jilly reaches into the stocking, sliding her hand to the toe. She withdraws a flashing tablet and they all lean in to peer at it. At Jilly's touch, the timer stops and the screen illuminates. The background photo shows a group of girls, hugging.

'That's us,' says Jane.

'Day we got our A-Level results,' says Emma.

'Who took it?' says Tatum. 'The photographer must have been outside the school.'

Jilly swipes the screen. 'There's one app. Instagram.' She taps it to open. 'It's following one account. Slebwatch?'

'Celebrity gossip,' Jane says.

'Obsessed with Mallory,' says Emma.

'They're streaming something, look.' Tatum reaches over Jilly's arm and hits WATCH LIVE.

◆ ◆ ◆

2003

Mad World

The Christmas Number One blasts from the pub. *Going nowhere, going nowhere.* The girls will never get served, not even with fake ID. Maybe Jilly looks old enough. Only seventeen, but she's got this middle-aged air about her, like she should have a wax jacket and a Range Rover. She'll have Labradors one day.

I'm holding two parcels. One is my Secret Santa present and the other is an envelope full of dog mess. A message. The same message that gets deposited on my doorstep any time I speak to Christopher—Kit—who won't make eye contact these days, as though we're hostages and he doesn't want to be the first one to get shot. I know it's her. My mum knows it's her. But my mum works for Jilly's mum, and Jilly's mum is bosom buddies with Kit's mum, so...

Quiet permission. That's what the counsellor calls it. When adults and peers do nothing about envelopes of dog mess.

Inside the pub, the girls spot a table in the snug. They have drinks. Fair play to Jilly, she got served. She lays the Secret Santa stocking on the table. I should go in and show them the envelope. They should know what she's like. I step forward—

But then I stop. Three boys join them. And then Kit. He kisses Jilly as they sit down. At last, he got to join Secret Santa again.

The song blares as someone exits the pub: *Children waiting for*
—

'—the day they feel good,' I sing under my breath.

I'm always waiting. Waiting to pass my A-Levels. Waiting for life to start. Waiting for the day I feel good? I can't wait any longer.

I dump the parcels in the bin on the way to the bus stop. I'm going to stay at my aunt's. This is the last time I'll see them. *Going nowhere*, I hum, *going nowhere*.

◆ ◆ ◆

2020

Fairy lights gilt the wet pavement outside the restaurant. As she gets out of the cab, the doorman of *L'Haut Pavot* tries to help Mallory step over a huge puddle, but she waves him away. She wants nothing to block the view.

While her companion pays the driver, she arranges the thigh-high slit in the front of her silk dress. This is her signal to the paparazzo to start live streaming #Slebwatch #Mallory #SecretSantaTV

Her companion slides a hand around her back.

'Kit—' she says.

'Hate that,' he says.

'Christopher.' She turns up her face. He hesitates a moment and then lands a full kiss on her mouth.

Behind his head, she checks her watch. This is her signal to the cyclist. Exactly forty-eight minutes since she left the pub. The device in the stocking has gone off. Her audience awaits...

The cyclist advances. Mallory resists Christopher's nudge toward the restaurant and holds him for a second on the edge of the kerb. The bike races through the puddle. Even though she is expecting a soaking, the cold takes her breath away and her scream is genuine.

The paparazzo comes closer, phone aloft.

Mallory spreads her arms to reveal to Christopher the extent of the damage she has suffered; water glistens her thighs, silk outlines her crotch, the dress clings to her breasts.

The doorman brings a cloth. Christopher kneels at Mallory's feet to wipe her down. A group of girls appear and scream 'Mallory!'

'Who's your date?' yells the pap.

Mallory beams a celebrity smile. 'I've been waiting for the right guy all my life!' She puts a crooked finger beneath his chin and raises him to his feet. 'This is Christopher.'

Jo Furniss

After spending a decade as a broadcast journalist for the BBC, Jo Furniss gave up the glamour of night shifts to become a freelance writer and serial expatriate. Originally from the United Kingdom, she spent seven years in Singapore and also lived in Switzerland and Cameroon. Jo's debut novel, *All the Little Children*, was an Amazon Charts bestseller, and was followed by *The Trailing Spouse* and *The Last to Know*. Connect with her via Facebook (JoFurnissAuthor) and Twitter (@Jo_Furniss) or through her website, www.jofurniss.com or her Amazon author page: bit.ly/JoFAmazon.

A DOG IS FOR LIFE, NOT JUST FOR CHRISTMAS

Robert Scragg

'Of course we can't bloody keep her,' Mum says. 'She's not our dog. That man who put the posters up, he'll be worried sick.'

'But muuuum. She was my Christmas present.'

'But mum nothing. We're calling that number, and she's going back. Simple as that. And just because you dragged her back here on Christmas Eve doesn't make her a present.'

'She likes it better here though,' I say, feeling a prickling behind my eyes as I look down at the she-in-question, also known as Lola. Worried eyes look up at me from under the table like she knows she's the cause of the argument. A snow-white Staffy, except for matching brown patches on each ear. Scruffy red collar around her neck, tiny dog-bone print pattern worn badly enough that it looks older then the dog. She's got the saddest eyes I've ever seen.

'We're calling him now, end of story. Tell her, Bill.'

Dad looks almost as sad as Lola. I know he wants her to stay almost as much as I do, but Mum usually gets what she wants.

'Your mum's right Maggie,' he says, patting my hand. 'Lola belongs to somebody else. Imagine how much they'll be missing her.'

'Not as much as I will if she goes back.' And suddenly, an idea hits me. So simple. 'Why don't we let Lola decide?' I say, wiping away the few tears that were blurring the edges, hoping Mum and Dad haven't spotted. I'm not a baby anymore, and twelve-year-olds shouldn't cry like this.

Mum's face softens, and she even manages a smile, but I can tell she thinks I'm just being silly.

'If you can get her to speak, and say she wants to stay, then that's fine.'

'I'm being serious, Mum. We can take her to the man, and we both call for her, and whoever she goes to gets to keep her.'

'Doesn't work like that pumpkin,' Dad says with a shake of his head. 'The man who put the poster up, Mr Russell, he owns Lola. We can't keep her. We just can't. We *could* maybe, have a look for a dog of our own though? Would you like that?'

'But I've got one already,' I say, hating how whingy I sound. 'And what if he's mean to her?' I'm feeling desperate now. 'What if she doesn't like it there, and that's why she ran away?'

'You're just being silly now, Maggie. That's...'

Mum doesn't finish what she's about to say. Instead, her eyes narrow to slits, that way they do any time she thinks I'm not telling the truth. And I'm not.

'Maggie, I'm going to ask you something, and I need you to be honest with me.'

I nod, worried by the looks I'm getting. I think she knows what I've done, even though I don't know how she could.

'When you found her in the park and brought her home, how did you know what her name was?'

'I didn't, I just thought she looked like a Lola.' I can feel my cheeks burning at the lie, and hope Mum doesn't notice.

'So how do you explain the fact that the reward poster calls her Lola as well? Was it just a lucky guess?'

Busted.

'Mum, I didn't...'

She raises a hand, pointing her finger at me like a magic wand, and I half expect her to shout *Expelliarmus* and drive the lie right out of my head.

'The next words out of your mouth better be the truth, or I'm marching out of here with that sorry looking thing and taking her home this instant.'

The sorry-looking thing is looking from me to Mum and back again, trying the sad eyes on both. Mum seems immune, but every time Lola looks at me, I feel my heart break a tiny bit more.

'I did find her wandering in the park, honestly...'

'But?'

I don't want to admit the next part, cos I know it'll make Mum angry, but I'm worried if I don't, she'll shout at me anyway.

'But I did see a man there with her, looking for her. He's not a nice man, Mum, I've seen him there loads and he hits her. I even saw him kick her once, so I took the tag off her collar when I found her.'

'You did what?' Mum gasps.

'Why didn't you just tell us Maggie?' Dad asks, and as he reaches over to rub my shoulder, I start to cry. Can't help it. Hate it. Hate the lump that I just can't swallow down. Hate the stringy snots that I smear away with the back of my hand.

It's like Lola knows I need help, and she shuffles forwards, resting her head between my knees, doing the same long slow blinks that she uses to beg for treats.

'To be fair, she is a very nervous dog,' Dad says to Mum. 'You've seen how she flinches if you move too fast when you want to pet her. That's a sign they've not been treated well.'

Mum's face isn't as red now, as if anger is leaking out.

'Even if that's true, love, and I hope it isn't, we still can't keep somebody else's dog. If we see him do it again, I'll even help you ring the RSPCA yourself, how's that?'

'But that means he has to hit her again before he gets in

trouble! That's not fair!'

Lola nudges her nose further into my knees, and anything else I try and say is lost between sobs.

◆ ◆ ◆

When Mum opens the door, the man looks as mean as I remember. Nose as steep as a ski slope and long narrow teeth that belong on a rat. Rat-faced Mr Russell. He smiles when Mum hands over Lola's lead, but it looks wrong on his face, like it's drawn on, not real. He gives the reward money to Dad, with fingers stained a browny-yellow from cigarettes, just like Grandad. He's got more bracelets around his wrist than anyone I've ever seen. Some leather, others those rubber charity type ones. Some I recognise, some I don't. He says thank you to me for finding Lola. Tells us how he lives alone, and she's his only friend. That can't be true. The friend part at least, cos you don't hit your friends. I kneel down to give Lola a cuddle, biting my bottom lip to stop myself from crying, so hard I wonder if it's bleeding.

I pull back and her tongue slurps one last slippery trail across my cheek, and just like that, she's gone. I race up to my room, press my nose against the window, breath fogging up the glass, as I watch him open his car boot. He points inside, and I expect he's asking her to jump in. My heart breaks all over again as she flattens her ears, and looks back at the house, like she can see me, and she's blaming me for being back with him. He speaks a second time, teeth bared like the giant rat he is, as he leans down towards her. She backs up half a step, and as he reaches for her, her tail tucks in fear, as if it's been blown underneath by a strong wind. He practically throws her in the boot, and even then, she leans forward to try and lick him, but he pushes a palm against her nose, shoving her further inside. All she wants to do is give people kisses, and he won't even let her do that.

I'm crying so hard that I don't know if my nose will ever stop running. You shouldn't hurt dogs, or any animal for that matter. You just shouldn't. Anyone mean enough to hurt an animal deserves something mean to happen to them. I'm never leaving my bedroom again. Ever.

◆ ◆ ◆

Three days. That's how long it takes me to believe that God exists for real. Three days after that horrible man shoved Lola in his boot, my prayers are answered. I'm in the back garden, making a snowman. Two splinters of wood from the fence for his teeth. A pair of tiny pebbles for eyes. I'm imagining this is Lola's owner, deciding whether to knock his head off first, or throw stones at his belly, when I hear the noise.

It starts as a soft scratching, like someone's rubbing against the garden gate. Then I hear a whimper, and my eyes pop wide with hope. I've barely opened the gate when Lola forces her way through the crack and before I know it she's planted both paws against my shoulders and licks my face like I'm covered in beef gravy. No idea how she got away, never mind found her way back here, but I don't care. She's here. That's all that matters. She's home.

After a glorious few minutes reunion, I realise, we can't stay out here like this. If Mum sees Lola, she'll just call that man again. Dad'll probably do the same to avoid getting in Mum's bad books. We creep through the kitchen, past the living-room door, where Mum and Dad sit watching some boring Christmas film, and up the stairs. My heart is beating too hard, it feels like it's whacking against the inside of my chest, and every creaky stair cries out, telling tales on me, but we make it in one piece thanks to my finger hooked into her collar to stop her scampering off.

Next comes Operation Snackage. An easy trip down to the kitchen, followed by a nervous trip back up, plate piled with peanut butter sandwiches for the pair of us. My dressing gown plus two pillows will do for a cosy corner for Lola. Those sad dark eyes fix on me as soon as I close my door. I tear one sandwich in half, and it's gone in a single swallow. The other half follows a few seconds later, and I giggle as she runs her tongue around her teeth, peanut butter stuck to them like brown toothpaste. I'm just so happy she's back, that I'll give her anything she wants.

The happiness only lasts another half an hour though. I hear the phone ring, and a minute later, heavy footsteps trudge up the stairs, stopping at my door. Sounds like Dad, and sure enough, the voice that follow the knock is his. I try and lure Lola under my bed with promises of licking the crumbs from my plate, but as soon as Dad comes in she's out like a shot, fussing around his ankles, flipping onto her back, begging for a tummy tickle. Not like I thought I'd be able to keep her stashed away forever, but still, worst attempt at hiding ever.

The man is back at our door soon after, muttering about how he'll have to keep a closer eye on her, thanking us again. He's smiling at me, but it's only his mouth, not his eyes. They just look mean and cold. This time, when I race to the window, he's dragging her, the lead looking more like a pole, stretched so tight, collar biting into the fur around her neck. Lola's trying to sit down, but he's too big, too strong, and her paws can't do anything but slide on the slush-stained ground. They disappear, leaving only dirty drag marks in the driveway.

◆ ◆ ◆

This time I pray to Santa, asking for my Christmas present back, for good this time. Santa must be more powerful than God, cos this time it only takes a day. I've been leaving the back gate open, just in case she found her way here again, and sure enough, she creeps through it just after lunch, just her nose peeking in first, like she's learned from last time that I'm the only one she can trust. This time though, Mum is the garden, scattering salt on the icy path. She rolls her eyes, bends down, patting her leg, and Lola, the over-friendly fool that she is, runs right up to her, licking her under her chin, around her neck, across both hands, so much that when Mum wipes her hands on her jeans, it leaves smudged wet trails.

Dad looks almost as sad as I feel when he picks up the phone to call the man.

He starts talking, telling the man we've found his dog, again, but stops, and his face makes a funny frown.

'Oh, okay… Yes, I see… No, no. That's fine… Yes, we can hang on to her for now… Yes, of course…'

When he's done, he has a weird look on his face. 'Maggie, sweetheart, why don't you take Lola up to your room to play for a bit?'

'What's wrong, Bill?' I hear Mum ask as Lola and I head out of the kitchen and start up the stairs. 'When's he coming for her?'

'He isn't.'

Dad sounds funny, and I hook a finger under Lola's collar, stopping halfway up, to listen in.

'What do you mean he isn't?'

'That was the police who answered his phone,' Dad says. 'He's dead.'

'He's what?'

'Dead.' Dad says again, in a voice like he's trying to whisper, but failing badly.

'Oh my god. How? What happened?'

'They think he had some kind of allergic reaction. They've asked if we can hang on to Lola for now until they see if he has any family.'

Lola and I creep up the last six stairs, careful not to step on the middle of the really creaky one, second from top. Dad said we have to keep Lola, and I'm so happy I could burst, but there's a weird feeling in my tummy. Something's slithering around inside like I've swallowed a snake. I never thought he'd actually die. I just thought the peanut butter would give him a nasty rash when Lola licked him, just like Noah at school. He's got one of those rubber bracelets around his wrist too that tell you about his nut allergy, just like the rat-faced man, and Noah just comes out in big itchy red blotches if he eats any.

If mum was angry at how I lied about finding Lola, she'd be

fuming if she knew about this.

'We can't tell Mum,' I say, closing my bedroom door, reaching down to ruffle her ears. She follows me over to my bed, leaping up, turning tight circles on the duvet, then flopping down by my pillow.

'Besides,' I say to Lola, smiling as she licks my hand, 'people who are mean to animals deserve something mean to happen to them.'

She blinks her agreement. That's settled then. Our little secret.

Robert Scragg

Robert Scragg had a random mix of jobs before taking the dive into crime writing; he's been a bookseller, pizza deliverer, Karate instructor, HR manager and football coach. He lives in Tyne & Wear, and is part of the Northern Crime Syndicate crime writers group. Find him on Twitter @robert_scragg or on his website www.robertscragg.com. For more books by Robert, go to his Amazon author page: bit.ly/RobertSAmazon.

DRIVING HOME FOR CHRISTMAS

Rachael Blok

'Mulled wine?' Lily drinks it like it's pink lemonade. 'I've put a film on in the back for the kids. Die Hard.'

'Lily!'

'Just kidding. It's *Home Alone*. Is there veg you want chopping?'

My sister-in-law eyes the huge Brussels sprout tree lying on the quartz counter, hanging firmly onto her glass.

'Don't worry,' I say, waving my hand. 'Jocelyn will help once she's back.' I glance at the clock on the wall and think of how much I've missed my daughter. 'They should be here soon. Ben left a while ago.'

'Train's probably late. You know, three snowflakes on the line and it all grinds to a halt. Plus, it's Christmas Eve—busy. Pete's already said he'll be late. He talked about taking the day off but only managed the afternoon, after the pub trip. He's never missed a work drink in his life.' She rolls her eyes. 'You picked the sober brother. Clever you. You'd think owning the company would give them both a bit of freedom. But only Ben seems to act like it.'

I smile, and flick the fairy lights on in the kitchen. The sky is heavy outside. 'I hope Jocelyn caught the train. She sent a text saying battery was low, but she'd charge it in the carriage. But it's dead when I call. Bet she couldn't get near a socket.'

'Mince pie? Sod the diet. Don't worry, Em. They must be almost here.'

The snow falls like confetti outside. The trees are slowly disappearing into the white Oxfordshire fields. The gravel on the driveway is barely visible. A bell rings from somewhere, and I hear music starting up.

'Bloody carol singers.' Lily rises. 'Stay here. I'll go.' She brushes a few crumbs from her white cashmere jumper. I recognise it as the same one I've bought her for Christmas, wrapped under the tree.

'A tenner OK?'

I shrug and remember Jocelyn singing with the Brownies when she was young. She was planning to join the choir at university, but singing is still off the list—all that breathing. At least she'd been able to go, part online, part in person. She'd stayed after the end of term to finish some work, she'd said. But she hasn't been home since October. It's been a long one.

'Mummy?' Zac enters, trailing his green blanket. 'Albie told me Santa doesn't exist?' His round eyes glisten and are edged with panic.

I hunker down. 'Albie is being mean. And you know what, if Santa hears Albie saying that, he'll get nothing in his stocking tomorrow. Here, have a chocolate penguin, and one for Sara.'

He takes the chocolate in a chubby fist, and I don't think about the state of the sofa. Albie is almost ten and has inherited Pete's tendency towards jokes that he calls funny and others might call cruel. Lily hadn't wanted to send Albie to boarding school, but Pete had insisted. I remember his tiny face when he went away… He'd come back angry.

Zac and Sara arrived in their twinned glory six years ago. Jocelyn is mine from way before Ben. A surprise during my first year at uni. Pete had joked about that enough.

Only joking. Only joking.

I'd asked Lily if she'd planned on anymore, when Albie was about two.

I think the pregnancy weight was hard enough to get off once, wasn't it, Lils? Pete had answered for her.

'All done! I gave twenty. They're collecting for a women's refuge.' Lily tops her the mulled wine. 'Shall I put some songs on? '*Driving Home for Christmas*'?'

I smile and glance through the window. The snow is thicker. They should definitely be back.

'Come on!' Lily loops her arm through mine and picks up a box of truffles. 'Let's sit down for a bit.' She pulls me into the lounge where the fire is lit and four stockings are pinned. The smell of Christmas tree is like a filter in the room—every object seems covered with a shine, and the huge boxes with ribbons spill from beneath the branches.

'So good of you to host,' Lily says, lying her head back. She's holding a glass of champagne in her hand; she opened a bottle last night, after they'd arrived. Or maybe two.

◆ ◆ ◆

The hammering on the door is loud.

Lily sits up sharply. 'What's that? Bit loud for carol singers.'

Banging again.

The faint sound of, 'Mum!'

'Jocelyn!'

I skid on the wooden floor in socks, pulling at the front door. It flies open, the wreath banging against the wood, and snow swirls in on a cold blast. 'Jocelyn!'

There is blood on her face, and she's not wearing a coat.

'Mum! It's Ben. Oh, Mum!' She's crying, pulling me out. 'Please. Call an ambulance. We had a crash. At the end of the drive.'

'I'm dialling!' Lily shouts. 'You go!'

I grab a coat from the wall, and pull on boots, chase after Jocelyn.

'What happened?' We run into the freezing wind.

'He was turning into the drive. There must have been ice!' Her dark hair has come loose from its ponytail and lies wetly against her back.

'You're bleeding!' I shout, but she doesn't slow.

'It's nothing—I banged my head. The bag blew up though; I'm fine. Please, Mum, hurry.'

The driveway is longish. Maybe 100 metres. We sprint through the deepening snow like we're in the winter Olympics.

I see the car, bonnet crushed. It's slid into the tall oak that bends over the start of the drive.

'Oh, Mum. It's all my fault. If anything happens to Ben!' Jocelyn is crying.

'Ben!' I run towards him. The car door is partly open. The airbag has blown, but Ben's eyes are closed. He has blood on the corner of his face, and he stirs as I put my hand on his brow.

'Can you hear me? Ben, it's me, Emma. Can you hear me?'

'Emma?' His voice is faint. Less than a whisper. It sounds like a prayer. 'Jocelyn?'

'She's OK. The ambulance is on its way. Oh, Ben. What happened? You've taken that turn a million times!'

'Is Jocelyn OK?' he says again.

'They're almost here!' Lily is running towards us. She has no coat and the white jumper hangs heavy now, weighted with snow. Her blonde hair flies behind her, and her face is pale. She almost disappears into the background. I see her more vividly than I have for years. She's been disappearing for such a long time. I've been blind.

'This could be them. Apparently, there's been an accident near one of the pubs. A few ambulances were sent out. This one was nearby, wasn't needed.' She looks at the car. 'Christ. How did it happen?'

'Auntie Lily, I'm so sorry.' Jocelyn throws her arms around her, and cries on her shoulder. I briefly wonder why Jocelyn needs to apologise. Lily strokes her back, quietening her. 'Shhh, it's OK. He'll be OK.' Her eyes look to me over Jocelyn's shoulder. They ask if Ben will be OK, but his eyes are opening now.

'Shit, my leg hurts.' He lifts his hand to his face. 'Do I still look pretty?' he asks, sounding more like himself.

'Oh my God, Ben!'

'I'm OK. My leg hurts. Hang on.' He winces. 'I can wiggle my foot. Maybe it's just jarred.'

'The car looks almost buried! It must have been snowing harder than I realised,' I say, chattering about anything, holding his hand. 'And the train was on time. I've been worried... I should have gone.'

'Em, we're OK. Is that them?'

A siren sounds, and slowly, the flashing lights appear through the snowfall like lights on a Christmas tree.

I stand back, to let them in, and I grab Jocelyn, hold her tight. My baby girl, shivering, thin. 'Have you been eating?' I say.

'Honestly, Mum!'

◆ ◆ ◆

'I'll stay with the kids,' Lily says. 'I won't say anything. Call when you know.'

'Will do.' I hug her before I climb in the back of the ambulance. 'Thank you.'

'I'll stay off the wine. But only until you're back.' She makes an attempt at a grin, and I'm grateful.

Jocelyn grips my hand on the ride in, and later, as we wait for Ben in X-ray, she says, 'I'm sorry. Mum, I'm sorry. It was my fault. It was all my fault.'

'Don't be silly, Ben was driving. Not you. He knows how to drive.'

'Yes, but...' She stops. 'Mum. Ben said not to tell you. But I'm going to have to. I can't not. I know I haven't been home much...' She stops again.

'Ben said not to tell me? What? What is it?' I flush with heat, then immediately shiver. 'Jocelyn, tell me.' I keep my voice steady.

'Mrs Hamilton? Your husband is out of X-ray. The leg's not

broken but he's had a bleed into his knee joint, so he'll have to rest. But everything is clear. He's been very lucky.' The doctor smiles. 'It's not the first accident we've had in today. This snow takes everyone by surprise, every time.'

'Thank you.' I stand, wanting to throw my arms around this doctor, who doesn't look much older than Jocelyn. But we're still not really hugging strangers, and it would make a bit of a mockery of the masks we wear. 'Thank you so much!'

'He should be ready to go home soon. He's just getting dressed. Did you have that cut looked at?' The doctor looks at Jocelyn, and she touches her face, nodding. 'It's not mine. It's Ben's blood; it's my dad's.'

'Happy Christmas.' The doctor smiles and leaves, and I'm still wondering if I will want Ben home, after what Jocelyn has to say. The hairs on my arms stand ready, and I know that if Ben has done anything to hurt her, I will kill him. I can't imagine it, though. My Ben. Father to our twins.

'Tell me, sweetheart. Tell me now. Did Ben do something to you?'

'No! Nothing like that. Not Ben! No... It's something I did. I told him. It's why the car crashed. Mum...' She's crying now, and her shoulders shake. 'Mum, I wanted to tell you but I couldn't work out how. I knew you'd... Well. I didn't want...'

The phone rings, and it's Lily. I put my hand on Jocelyn's face, wiping her tears with my thumb, and with the other hand I lift the phone. 'It won't be long. We'll head home—'

'Emma. I can't believe it.' Lily's voice is quiet. Cold.

'What is it?' I spin, as though turning away will protect Jocelyn from more bad news. 'Is it the twins? Has something happened?'

'The police are here. It's Pete.'

'What? What happened?'

'Em, he's dead. He was found dead in a road. Outside a pub.'

'God, Lily. No! Was he driving?'

'No. They said he walked outside to meet a woman. She waved at him from the other side of the road. It was snowing, so no one really saw her properly. But he must have been hit by a car.'

I think of Pete, lying in the snow. Dead. Can he be dead? 'But which woman? Did the car stop?'

Lily's voice is faint. 'No. A hit and run. It's so quiet out there. There's no CCTV. No one really saw, and the woman's disappeared. Christ, he's dead, Emma. I've got to identify his body.'

'We'll be home in less than twenty minutes. Do nothing until I get there.'

◆ ◆ ◆

The taxi sails past the crashed car, crumpled up against the oak tree, and Lily is standing in the doorway, with two officers. They look apologetic.

Lily simply shakes her head as I take her in my arms.

The officers stand back. 'We thought we should stay, until you got here. So sorry for your loss.'

Ben hobbles over on crutches, and Jocelyn walks past, head bowed. 'I'll look after the kids. You go with her, Mum.'

'Do we have to go now?' I ask the officers.

But Lily answers. 'I've asked if I can go. I need to see him. Please. I'd like to get it over with. Will you come with me?'

'Lily,' Ben says, and puts one arm around her awkwardly, resting his other on a crutch.

She shakes her head. 'I can't... No comfort. Not yet.'

◆ ◆ ◆

An officer offers to drive us back, and it isn't until we're almost at the house that Lily says, 'He must have been having an affair... Then when he was hit... Maybe she was married too and didn't want to be found with him? I've half suspected.'

I put my hand on hers.

'He would say he was going out for the day. He said he'd pop up to take Albie out for lunch. Even Jocelyn. He always managed to do it in a way that excluded me. But it was all sham. He was just meeting this other woman.'

I squeeze her hand.

The car stops and the officer offers us a last round of condolences.

Walking toward the large wreath, the fairy lights around the house, I am hit with the truth of Pete being gone. Christmas dinner: no snide comments, no squeezes in the kitchen, or hugs that are a little too tight; Ben not having to apologise for his brother.

I silence the voice of betrayal. He is dead. And Lily and Albie are grieving.

I turn the key in the lock, pause. 'Pete said he went up to take Jocelyn out for lunch?' I say. I hadn't known this.

Lily nods, her white face paler still. She looks exhausted. 'I think just the once, towards the start of term. I thought she would have said? I didn't want to ask you. If he hadn't gone, I didn't want to have it confirmed. I've let a lot slide. He was...' She steps into the house, past me. 'Telling Albie will be hard. I'll do it now. But you know what? He won't have to go back to that bloody school now. Not anymore. It's over, Em. It's all over. Christ, don't tell anyone, but I'm glad.'

I follow slowly. My mind unwraps the day: takes off the bow, the paper... The box inside the box. I think of Jocelyn's face. Her tears. She's lost weight. She'd not come home. Ben crashing the car...

In the kitchen, Jocelyn is showered and changed, but she still looks cold. I want to put my arms around her, but I wait for a second. I look at her carefully, then I put on the kettle, and ask her, without looking at her, giving her a moment of grace.

'Sweetheart, can you tell me now? What you wanted to tell me?'

She says nothing. I pour water on a tea bag; open a box of biscuits, and I sit on a barstool, next to her. I dunk a biscuit in my tea, and push them towards her, saying, 'He's dead. Pete's dead. They don't know what happened. There were no witnesses. And no one saw the woman clearly, from the other side of the road. The snow was heavy.'

Jocelyn takes a biscuit, thick with chocolate.

'Maybe he deserved it,' I try. Then I wait.

She says nothing.

'Sometimes, people do. Sometimes, if someone does something truly terrible, then I think maybe...' I look at her. My blood boils, but I swallow the fire. I wait.

'He came to see me, Mum. To take me out for lunch. I didn't really think... Well, it was odd, but, you know. He bought wine. Took me somewhere fancy. Drove me back to the house, then asked to see inside. The others were at uni... I didn't...' She looks down at her tea. The biscuit has soaked through and half of it has fallen in.

There are a million things I want to say. To scream. I say nothing.

'He didn't... Not completely. He tried. I got out. I ran away. He was gone when I went back. I waited for Amy to finish lectures. She told me to go to the police, but I couldn't. What would it do to Auntie Lily? To Albie? But I was terrified about coming back. I had to see him. To face him. Before tomorrow.'

I force myself to take a drink. I sit. The things I would do to that man if he was still alive.

'I had a panic attack in the car. I told Ben. I was so upset... He knew which pub Pete was in. We went. I waved to him. Then when he was crossing the road, Ben drove... It's why he crashed the car. He said it would give us an alibi, and also with the car crumpled up, no one would think of checking it for...'

In my head, I thank Ben, offer him my everything. *Take everything for the safety of my daughter. Take it all.*

'Ben made me get out first. He said he'd have to drive fast enough to smash it, but that new cars crumple fast.' She cries.

Then she looks at me, and I see Zac's same glistening eyes looking back, wishing a chocolate penguin would fix it all.

'Do you hate me, Mum? Ben said I didn't have to tell. Said it could be our secret, if I wanted. But I had to tell you.'

'Jocelyn, I just wish I'd got to him first.' I wrap her up in my arms.

Snow gusts up against the window, and the lights above the oven blink out their Morse code of festivity. Blood can lie under the snow. We will wrap up our secrets, tie them tight.

Home for Christmas.

Rachael Blok

Rachael Blok is author of the psychological crime series, set in St Albans, where Dutch DCI Maarten Jansen unpicks the murders that occur. *Under the Ice* and *The Scorched Earth* are out now. *Into the Fire* will be published in April 2020 by Head of Zeus. Find her on Twitter @MsRachaelBlok, or on her website www.rachaelblok.com. For more books by Rachael, go to her Amazon author page: bit.ly/RachaelBAmazon.

SMITHEREENS

Dominic Nolan

First time I saw Santa, he came to Col's bottle shop to give gifts to the kids, and left on a Honda with a beautiful woman on the back. When they peeled away down the street, some parents asked what was wrong with him and why was someone like that allowed to be Santa anyway.

Next time I saw him, a year later, he didn't have the bike and there was no woman. He was lying out in the bush, drunk, with a fat lip and a cut over his eye. It was Christmas Eve, and four weeks later I watched Terry kill him.

◆ ◆ ◆

We'd been friends since playschool, Terry and me, one of those things it didn't seem either of us had a choice in. We shared age and a marooning in the Wheatbelt.

Where I was the type who shied from compliments and received gifts as if they were death threats, Terry wasn't just good at receiving things, he delighted in taking them. He wanted everything you had. Sometimes it worked out fine if you gave him it, but sometimes I knew he needed to take it.

Taking it was the thing.

◆ ◆ ◆

Hand like a blade across his eyes, Terry squinted against the sun.

'Where'd you leave it?' I asked, picturing his cap slung on the post of his bed.

'Someone took it,' he lied. 'Thought we was going the woods.'

I looked about us. 'We are.'

'Not these woods. The real ones.'

We were on his father's land to see the sheep that died in the fire. The eucalypt stands crescenting his fields had been scorched, burning away the canopy and leaving columns of dark needles, the sun pitiless overhead.

How we'd pictured them, slouched on their knees, half-sunk in soft cinders with eyeless heads reared back and globs of hardened flesh hanging from the bones.

Wasn't like that. Crossing a cauterised region of burnt stubble, we passed miles of fencing lost to the flames, the sheep it had enclosed lying black and bloated on their sides, legs out stiff. White cracks in their darkened but surprisingly intact wool.

It had been better in our heads.

I took off my cap. 'Here, take mine.'

Terry wrinkled his nose; it had the wrong team on it. It was one of Col's old ones, and Terry didn't like the Swannies now Perth had a team in the big league. Col said dickheads like him were why there weren't fifty thousand in the Oval come September no more. Footie wasn't something I cared about, though I could fake it if I had to.

'Better than a headache,' I said.

He looked like he wasn't so sure.

I pulled up my tanktop's thin hood, tucking my longer hair away.

'Nothing but ash here. Let's go to the knob.'

That was the granite outcrop sprouting from the centre of a jarrah wood, south of town. Miles from his dad's farm, I could see him wrestling with the walk.

'Only if I carry it.'

I pulled the strap of the bolt action .22 higher on my shoulder. With the cap business and the dead sheep and now this walk, I knew I'd let him, but it would be better to make him take it.

'Give it, Alex.'

He made a grab and I dodged out the way. Terry was bigger, but I was nimble, coltish. I kept this up, dancing out of reach, before letting him catch me—didn't want him too mad. On the ground his weight pressed on me as he yanked the strap from my arm. Stayed on me like that, his thighs on mine.

Everything hummed with the smell of him.

His fringe fell and I could have sucked sweat from it, his face was that close.

Tuna from lunch on his breath.

Turning my head, he pushed my cheek into the dark earth, but not too hard. Red-faced and panting, he wiped perspiration away on his sleeve.

'Come on,' he said.

In those days I was working in Col's bottle shop. It was the only one in town, and given there were two churches—papists and Presbyterians—Col was fond of saying he was more in demand than Jesus. Four bridges destroyed by the fire along the highway to the next town closed the road indefinitely, leaving Baptists, and anyone who didn't want to buy their tinnies from Col, shit out of luck. He may as well have been the mayor.

I got in at sparrows to restack the shelves. Clean the floor. Do a stock-take. Col liked the counter, and was happy to let me leave early if everything else was done. Had a small TV behind there and gabbed to the regulars. He knew what everyone drank, and how much.

When he married Mum he said he was big into pest-hunting, but I never saw him take the rifle out. Never saw him do much that didn't involve the stool behind his counter or the couch at home. Kept it in the garage where he never parked the old HZ, and it was easy to take it from where it hung.

He never noticed.

◆ ◆ ◆

Terry sighted things as we walked.

Claimed to spot tammars and numbats, but I never saw them. When we got to the rusted railway carriage, he jumped up and, when he thought I couldn't see, cleared it like his old man's war stories about Phuoc Tuy.

The carriage was a staging post near the knob, home to stuff we'd kept there for years: books and magazines, matches, food sometimes. Nobody knows how the thing got there, out in the trees a good mile from the railway and going nowhere. The track still ran plumb through the middle of town, but nobody had ridden it in years. Just the occasional grain train to the big bins.

Good woods surrounded the knob, rich with jarrah and marri. Near the base of the granite was our place; away from paths or tracks, a bend in a creek where someone had tried tipping an old fridge into the water. It stood heeled in the sediment on the slow side. A giant jarrah had been felled above the bank, the stump as wide as a table, the reclining trunk up to our chests.

That's where I saw Santa again.

◆ ◆ ◆

Crushed tinnies lay about him like screwed-up poems.

The red Santa suit stood out even against the ochre earth. Terry cast his eyes round like maybe we'd stumbled into the wrong place. We'd never seen anyone else out there.

'He's dead.'

'He's breathing.'

Terry shrugged like that didn't matter. Creeping up slowly to the heaped man, he poked him with the humourless end of the rifle.

'Not moving.'

Crouching down, I took a good look.

'It's him.'

'No shit. How many Santas you suppose there are?'

Col had hired the bloke the previous year—do himself up in a Santa costume and hand out presents from a sack to the kids. Done it in towns all through the Wheatbelt, the fella said. Seemed to go off okay until he left and Moses Tooth claimed to recognise him.

Tooth wasn't strictly a local, only having lived in town the twenty years. From the coast, he was running his late father's butcher shop into the ground when a developer offered him good money for it, so he retired out here for reasons that have never been clear to anyone, least of all Tooth himself.

He recognised Santa from his old neighbourhood, knew him as Ray Gabb, and said for a fact he was not only a troublemaker but half a boong to boot. Ray had been due to return as Santa that year, but it seemed the good townsfolk hadn't been so welcoming this time.

A single uncrumpled can stood near Ray's head. Terry toed it gently before picking it up, placing it on our tree stump. Standing barely ten yards off, he took aim.

'Where's the ammo?'

I'd taken it all out of my bag before leaving home.

'Isn't any.'

He looked at me. 'What?'

'Thought there was some in my bag, but there wasn't.'

He shook his head. 'Bullshit. There has to be.'

He took my bag, unzipped it and rooted through.

'You checked the pockets?' he said. He took stands like this, prepared to deny anything. His face fell. 'Nothing.'

'Got my beer?'

The voice, deep and jarring, cut through me. Terry almost fell over, spinning round and raising the rifle at Ray.

'Don't you move!'

Sitting there, elbows on his knees, red and white hat still on his head, he said, 'You just asked your mate for ammo.'

'No, I didn't.'

'Could do with a swig of that beer.'

Terry walked to the stump. Looking at Ray, he knocked over the can with the butt of the rifle. Ray didn't blink. He stared at me.

'I know you. From the bottle-o.'

'Work there.'

'Yeah?'

'Yeah.'

'Fella runs it's a dog.'

I shrugged, not needing telling about Col. He rose unsteadily to his feet and stumbled off toward the creek, the bell on his hat tinkling softly as he moved. The bank was three or four feet down to the gravel bar where the fridge was. He opened it and took out another tinny.

'Last one,' he said.

'Col sold you those?' I said.

He smiled. 'Bit of a misunderstanding when I arrived. Took these as a souvenir.'

'Where's your bike?' Terry said.

'Gone.'

'They take it off you?' I said.

He shook his head. 'Nah. Lost it long before I come here.'

'There was a woman with you last time you come through.'

'She went about the same time as the bike, mate.'

Terry lowered the rifle.

'How'd you get here?'

'Truckie.'

'Why you out in the woods?'

'Seemed sensible to leave town. Bit strapped for cash, though.'

'Moses Tooth reckons you're a blackfella.'

Ray laughed, shook his head. 'Hadn't seen that old dog for twenty-five years. Some odds running into him in a place like this.'

He clambered up the bank and sat on the stump, chugging the

beer.

'How'd you become a Santa?' I asked.

'Same way every Santa does. Stole the coat and hat from the old one.'

'Did not.'

'Fella I did a stint with at Wooroloo, reckoned he did it to case places. Get to sit around all day figuring things out. Talk to the owners, see the general doings.'

'That worked?'

'He was in Wooroloo, what d'you think?'

'You made off with Col's grog, at least.'

'Daring heist, aye.'

'Where you sleeping?'

He looked heavenwards. 'Not going to rain.'

'Bit blowie, maybe. You should go to the train.'

'You'll do a perish out here, mate. The train'll see you right,' Terry said, like it was his idea.

It was an open carriage with pairs of two-seat benches facing each other either side of a narrow aisle. Some of the windows still had curtains, and Ray pulled the ratty drapes closed as he went along.

'How d'you suppose it got here?'

'Slowly,' I said.

◆ ◆ ◆

Ray had been busy.

Next day we found the carriage deserted, and the fridge was gone from beside the creek. The empty tinnies had been gathered into a pile beside the stump. Terry straightened them out as best he could and stood them along the downed trunk.

He held his hand out, wiggling his fingers. I dropped a bullet into his hand—you didn't give Terry any more than one at a time. He struggled with the mechanism.

'You cleaned it?'

I shrugged, taking it from him and making out it was tricky to load.

'Think there was something caught in there. Should be right now.'

I kept behind him as he took aim. From six yards, he missed.

'Coulda been walking about back there,' Ray said from the side.

'I'd have seen you,' I said.

I always let a few things escape unseen from Col's bottle shop. Setting my backpack down, I lifted out the box of wine.

'Figured you could do with something.'

'Too right.'

Ray tore open the cardboard and drank straight from the goonbag. After a long, loud guzzle, he looked embarrassed.

'Didn't catch your name.'

'Alex. This is Terry.'

'I'm Ray.'

'Everyone knows that,' Terry said.

I offered Ray a paper bag.

'Made a sandwich too.'

He acknowledged me with his eyebrows and tucked in like he hadn't eaten for a month. By the time he was done, he'd put away half the wine and wore the loose smile of someone who believed themselves invulnerable.

'Where's the fridge?' I asked.

He showed us behind the fallen trunk. With sticks, he'd dug a hole and buried the fridge, facing up so it opened like a chest. Covered with branches and brushes of jarrah leaves, we'd never have found it.

'Why?' Terry said.

Ray shrugged. 'Boredom?'

He put the silver wine bag in it, then opened the door and removed it immediately.

◆ ◆ ◆

Ray was in a bad way—drunk and maudlin.

The goonbag was empty. He told us he had wasted his entire life and only held dear those who'd done worse. He spoke of a farmer's sweet daughter in Gidgegannup who made love to him under the stars. Blind drunk, they slept in a hollow among the wildflowers and he awoke to find it had rained and she'd drowned in an inch of water.

It was nothing to imagine him going on like that all night.

◆ ◆ ◆

The moon hung in tatters behind skeins of black clouds.

Gusted away, the sudden lighting of the land caused Ray to look up. With a gallon of plonk inside him, he'd staggered up onto the stump to piss at the dark, his sounds joining those of the creek water coursing. Tilting his head back proved an act of contortion too far and he toppled backwards off the tabletop, still clutching himself and arcing his water like a wild hosepipe.

The dull landing winded him and he lay in the mud of his own making, unable to gather himself. His once-red trousers bunched about his thighs, prick thumbing out of his undies. Expecting seashell pink, I was surprised by its darkness.

'We should go,' said Terry.

It was the sight of it that worried him. Take that away and all you had was a tumbled down derelict. Eyes closed, Ray breathed like a perishing elephant. I tucked him back into his jocks and with effort rolled him onto his side and into the lee of the fallen trunk, safe from the coming day's sun.

Emboldened by my action, Terry approached. Lightly, he raked the muzzle down Ray's back. Reaching his undies, he pushed them in until they snagged in his crack. Terry giggled.

He'd reached his limit early and left nowhere to go.

Collecting fallen honkynuts from a nearby bleeding marri, I made a heap beside Ray. I balanced one on his shoulder. Terry hijacked this game eagerly, placing the nuts in Ray's hair and on his neck, one with its valve cupped in his ear.

We left laughing.

◆ ◆ ◆

Ray was deep in his turps before we arrived.

I had a small bottle of blended rotgut he attacked on sight.

The subject of his blues for the day was his father, who'd lit out when he was a boy, name turning up in the papers from time to time; first for playing county footie up in Mukinbudin, and then for a burglary earning him a spell in Fremantle.

Later, Ray and his pal Wally had knocked over a hock shop masquerading as a jeweller's in Northam, and by chance came across a Central Wheatbelt premiership medal of his old man's in their haul. Now, this was serendipitous for sure, but not so much that there had to be a divine hand in it. Ray, though, he carried the thing around with him for years.

'I'd think about finding him. Handing the medal over. But I couldn't picture how that'd go, couldn't see what would happen beyond that. Sometimes it's better to look at the past. It's all there for you, every little piece of it blown apart. There'll always be worse things to come.'

Maybe because we came to see him, or for the grog we brought, he'd put on these performances. Looting his soul for blessings to give us.

Reaching out, he clutched Terry's arms to show how serious he was about this, and puked in the space between them. Terry scrambled backwards desperately, his bare legs vomit-splashed.

'Jesus! Why'd you do that?'

On his hands and knees, Ray groaned. He had nothing.

Terry cuffed him weakly on the top of the skull. Ray barely

noticed.

'Deserves more than that,' I said.

Terry looked at me, but I was staring at his legs.

Making a fist, Terry struck him hard round the side of the head.

'Fucken ear,' Ray cried.

'I dunno,' I said.

Terry was steaming. He punched Ray in the face, and he fell flat on his back. Grinning upwards, blood outlining his teeth. Terry hit him again and once more when he tried to get up, the wild punches of a dabbler in that sort of thing.

Swaying on his knees, Ray looked up pleadingly.

I knew his secret, what it was he wanted. Terry caught barely a glimpse in the corner of his eye, but gave it to him as best he could.

Part of the secret was not talking about it the next day.

◆ ◆ ◆

Ray knew a gnamma up north deep enough to jump into off a sixty-foot sheer rock face.

'Left the damn medal in my pocket making a leap. Still be down there somewhere. Be down there forever. Like those hands on the rock walls.'

You'd think there'd be a fidelity to stone, but even the earth will betray us. In as little as a hundred million years all of this will be unrecognisable. Nothing we know will remain.

◆ ◆ ◆

We sat around the dying tucker fire in discrete silences.

In vest and undies, Santa costume nowhere to be seen, Ray poked the embers with a stick he'd cooked wild roots on. However old he was, he'd arrived there bluntly. There was much wrong with him, but nothing as bad as Terry, who worked at a knee scab curling up like a scorpion's tail, placing the pickings on his tongue. I fetched the Santa hat from the train, feeling it would catalyse a more communal quiet.

At last I yielded up the bottles, unmarked blends of my own concoction as I was having to be canny with what I took from the store. There were cans of liquids in the garage Col told me to keep away from, warning they'd make me sick if I drank them. He wasn't wrong; took just long enough to polish off the bottles for Ray to turn.

He lay on his side, knees bunched as if gutshot.

Like a beast in frenzy, his eyes rolled.

He howled maddingly.

Terry got to his feet in a fright. 'Is he going to die?'

I was curious myself.

'Should we get someone?'

'Who would we get?' I said. 'Who would even care?'

Ray coughed up a cupful of blood.

'Jesus, we should do something.'

I watched closely, noting every little detail. Ray was offering us one last blessing, one I would return to again and again.

Terry began to cry when Ray suffered fits.

'Hold him,' I instructed.

He was unsure, but got Ray on his back and sat on his chest, pressing down on both shoulders. Ray vomited thick pink froth, tanking in his mouth and filling his throat.

'Should we roll him?' Terry said. His face was mucus slick.

I shook my head.

'Alex...'

I stared down into Ray's wayward eyes.

'Hold him steady.'

What can we teach the dead? Santa hat on his head, he looked less hemmed in by his plight.

◆ ◆ ◆

Dusk brimmed the woods.

Terry had the rifle.

'You got ammo?'
'For what?'
'Make it look like suicide.'
'How would the gun be explained?'
Terry was in over his head. I grabbed a leg.
'Help me with him.'
We dragged Ray behind the fallen trunk and opened up the fridge. The shelves were long gone and folded up a bit he fitted in there just so. I found his top and trousers hanging from a bush like battle flags, washed and left to dry. I tossed them in, plinking the hat's bell. We heaped over earth and scattered branches and other detritus.
'I never touched him,' I said.
Nobody found him for years.
Crop-saving rains broke the banks of the creek almost two decades later and washed away the soil, revealing the fridge to kids playing there afterwards. They opened the door and saw what was left of Ray, just bones and the outfit and hat, barely recognisable as red any longer.
A few people remembered stories about the visiting Santa Claus, a thief and a troublemaker and half a boong to boot. Said he must have climbed in to escape the night chill and couldn't get out. Nobody was too interested in why he hadn't been found before.

◆ ◆ ◆

Terry remained unseen in a bush.
Col was waiting out front with Mum, whistling and hollering.
'What have I told you about my rifle?'
He'd never once mentioned the rifle.
Snatching it from me, he grabbed a fistful of my t-shirt. Saw it in my eyes, what I thought of him.
'Oh, you're a bold girl, Lexie.'
I smirked and he slapped me round the back of the head. Falling forwards, I skinned my knee on the asphalt drive, but con-

cerned myself more with the neck of my tee, loose where he'd stretched it. Dragging me up, he drew his hand back again.

'She's in school tomorrow,' Mum said quickly. 'First day at big school.'

Col hesitated, then punched me in the belly.

Curled up on the floor I could see Terry peeking out behind the bush. It was all there for him, every little piece blown apart, but he was always thinking about other things.

His heart his lungs his prick.

Hard to say if things might have been different. Later, he drank a lot and talked in his cups. It's a trick of life that you march upon the end just as slowly as the next fella, yet might arrive years sooner.

He died in a mysterious fire.

What it was he wanted from me, I never knew.

And you, you prying cunts, what is it you want from me?

Dominic Nolan

Dominic Nolan is the author of the Abigail Boone thrillers, *Past Life* and *After Dark*, published by Headline. He lives in London but you can find him on Twitter @NolanDom. For more books by Dom, go to his Amazon author page: bit.ly/DominicNAmazon.

MISSTEPS

N.J. Mackay

I feel a wave of irritation as I scurry round the shops but force it away. I'm determined to make it a lovely Christmas. Besides, you cannot be cross with someone when they are suffering. I repeat this to myself several times a day. It's an illness, that's what you have to understand—what I have to understand—albeit one you can't see. It is the extra thing we live with now. An unwelcome visitor in our house, almost a person in its own right. I think of it as a quiet malicious thief. Stealer of time. Stealer of peace, stealer of energy.

I'd been looking forward to this year.

The last child gone—my time now.

Stolen.

Redundancy came for Jim at a time least expected. A few weeks of a sort of blind panic. Then settling into a cross silence. My outgoing lively husband retreated. First he set up a moody but defiant camp downstairs. Now he just stays in bed. The days have ticked by, becoming months, a year.

Depression the doctor says. Like a broken leg, though that would be easier. They know how to fix that. A plaster cast, which we could all scrawl our names on in different coloured sharpies.

More importantly, an end date. A rough idea of when improvements will happen. How that might look.

We were young when we met. Full of plans and ideas, he was studying for his degree as I was mine. University sweethearts. The thrill of the first relationship away from the prying eyes of parents. No curfews, no rules. Freedom and all it entailed. We hadn't been planning a child of course but one came along and, well... I'd finish studying later when the little one was older, at nursery or school.

Tentatively I'd suggested an alternative.

Unthinkable now. That it even crossed my mind and I feel a pang when I recall it. Lilly was wonderful, is wonderful. A young woman growing into herself. Older now than the age I was when she arrived. She seems impossibly unformed still, a colt on wobbly legs supported by us still but from a distance. The happy accident that changed my life, made me a mother. Defined what was to become my role for many years. All of the years to date.

My job back then, we decided, was to support him, this young man who found himself suddenly filled with a responsibility he hadn't banked on. We'd work hard. Get ahead. Get married when we had the time and the money.

I'd been terribly ambitious and the smartest girl in my school. I was studying law and whilst my peers struggled to soak in the information it was never a problem for me.

I'd go far.

That's the one thing I'd heard my whole life and I would. It was just a pause. Not a stop.

My mother cried when I told her and I felt my own heart lurch on that day. A little tremor or sadness replaced quickly by indignation.

We were young.

In love.

Jim was adamant that we'd make a go of it. Take this unexpected thing and make it into the start of a brilliant life.

He got his head down. Came out with a 2:1. If I felt a little moment of jealousy and the fleeting thought that I'd have got a first, it passed as fast as it came unbidden into my mind.

I didn't go back to finish when Lilly started school. By then I was pregnant again and along came Thomas, so Lilly wouldn't be an only child. When Thomas went into his reception class, bright as a button and full of energy, another child, unplanned.

I'd be lying if I said I hadn't had a little cry then once or twice. Behind closed doors and never in front of Jim or the little ones.

Tentatively again I'd suggested the alternative and he was appalled. He was doing well. We'd bought our first little place. We were on our way. Eventually we'd get married; why wouldn't we welcome another one?

Okay I said. I'd go back when this one started school. Before I knew it, a decade had passed in a blur of nappies and pushchairs. Sleepless nights, a split perineum and lax, unreliable pelvic muscles.

Jim was busy at work, never really had much time for the kids. But he paid the rent, then the mortgage. When I suggested I get a part-time job he'd laughed and said I was needed at home.

And I was, of course, book-bags and lunch boxes didn't pack themselves after all, and the admin. The piles and piles of child admin that three of them brought. Childcare for all of them meant me working was barely worth it. The sort of jobs I'd get with half a degree and no work experience made the balance laughable. I'd be paying someone else to work.

Jim needed down time of course. He was the one bringing in the cash, keeping us all afloat.

We never did have the wedding.

There wasn't a moment where there was the spare time. Or the spare money, but he took care of the practicalities, the finances, and I let him. My days were so packed with endless mindless chores it gave me one less thing.

Even when they were at school there was a lot of running around, plays to attend. Reading in various classes, helping out on school trips, and if you did it for one you had to do it for all.

One morning a woman at the school gates rushing off in smart shoes with neat hair and an air of purpose said how lucky that I didn't have to work. How nice it must be to be at home.

And I'd smiled and nodded. Numbly making my way back to fold the washing.

Lucky.

Head girl.

A star student.

Mother.

◆ ◆ ◆

The depression was hardly his fault. His company made changes and, it turned out, some of his colleagues were less than happy with his performance over the years. The more power he got, the less he did, they claimed. He was incredulous. Long lunches and leisurely dinners on trips away were networking for goodness sake. He got a reasonable amount in redundancy, but most of it was sucked up by Zach's university fees. We'd paid rent for one and two and would have to do the same for him. It wouldn't be fair otherwise. What Jim got wouldn't last forever. But it was fine. He'd find another job.

He didn't though. He looked for a bit, made some applications, and didn't even get to interview. He'd been at the same company so long, perhaps it would take time I'd said. He ignored me. Instead he sulked and drank and scowled. For the first time ever it was just the two of us and he was almost a stranger to me as I must have been to him. The big house, usually my domain, felt smaller with him in it. He went to bed for a few weeks. Then a month. He drank in the daytime, bleary-eyed and weary.

He was like this all year, the bank balance getting lower and lower. I'd managed to squirrel a little bit away over the years. Not much, because Jim never gave me large amounts—no need for the housekeeping. I hadn't told him about it, he was a lavish kind of man, prone to bouts of generosity, which were lovely but always made me a bit uncomfortable. The children loved the big gift days of course but then they didn't understand the cost of running a house on one income. I never really knew how well or not we were doing but assumed everything was fine.

Now they were grown, the children, and that was that. I suppose I'd thought of that money as mine. What I'd use to finish my degree. Get back into law. Though now we were struggling to cover our mortgage. I got a job seven months ago. In a law firm. I watch the young ones, just passed all their studying and think, *that could have been me.*

Silly really.

It wasn't me.

I was a middle-aged woman doing the filing and making the tea. With a husband secreted at home wrapped in a fuggy blanket of his own misery.

I'd get in and he'd be belligerent, sometimes drunk. We slept in separate rooms, had done for years, so mostly I tried to stay out of his way.

But the Christmas holidays were upon us, the children were coming home, and I was determined, absolutely adamant, that we'd make it a great day, a turning point for us.

I was running around the shops on a grey December Saturday morning like a woman possessed. I wasn't spending a fortune; we didn't have one. But each gift was thoughtful and considered. And that's what mattered wasn't it? It would be up to me to inject some cheer into it all. I wanted the children to come home and visit, though I could understand why they hadn't before. My daughter in particular had no time for what she deemed her father's 'antics'. I understood. I hardly wanted to be there myself most of the time. Certainly I didn't want to be using a day off to press into the thrum of shoppers but Jim wasn't up to it.

Besides he wouldn't know what anyone wanted.

◆ ◆ ◆

When I get home I am delighted to find that that he is up and dressed. Less delighted when he smiles sadly at me and sighs.

'Come on in, Philly.'

I say, 'Just give me a sec, these things aren't for prying eyes.'

With a forced smile. An expression I've learned to wear like a mask over the years.

Jolly.

Easy going.

Mild mannered.

Not the fiery girl from the debating society with the world ahead yet to conquer.

He's always called me that. Philly. He was the first person to do so and what I'd initially found endearing has begun to grate. Every time he says it, in my head I hear Phillipa.

I stash the bags in the cupboard under the stairs along with all of the other crap we've piled there over a lifetime.

He is in the kitchen. Standing with his back pressed against the side. Foot tapping, showing... impatience?

He runs a hand through his hair.

I say, 'You look better.' Tentative words, ones that dare to hope.

He nods, 'I am. Much so. I've ah... made some decisions.'

I say, 'Oh?'

Taking the one bag of perishables I start to unpack it. I slip by him to get to the fridge and he kind of side steps me. I start putting little wraps of cheeses away.

He snaps, 'God can you just stop.' I jump.

I close the door, turn to face him.

He says, 'Oh god. Look, the walls are closing in.' a favourite phrase of his. The thing he's found the absolute worst after redundancy has been being 'trapped in the house'. I've bitten my tongue, not pointed out that 'the house' was where I've whiled away the best years of my life. That I too knew of the trappedness he's talked of. But I haven't said anything.

You don't, do you?

I mean he did, obviously.

I didn't.

'Let's go, walk.'

'Alright.'

I still have my jacket on and follow him to the front door,

watch him slip his socked feet into his awful sandals that don't fit and always aggravate him, plus it's cold. I almost remind him to get his trainers but don't.

We live in a lovely house actually. Set in a rather remote area and backing onto beautiful cliff faces that sprawl as far as the eye can see. It was dreadful when the children were small, and we had a huge fence built around the garden. To stop them, especially Tom, running blindly too near the edge.

It was cheap. Worth a fortune now, as a little town was built at the bottom and a direct train to London was added at the station. Into Victoria in less than an hour.

Initially Jim stayed in London four nights a week, a trade-off for a house with so much space. Eventually he was able to commute daily. By that time the children were teenagers and I often thought I could have done with him in the evenings when they were small and bath time was anything up to two hours.

But still. The house is a blessing now. It's why I'm working my little job. It would be terrible to lose it, though I'm toying with the idea of us selling it.

We walk out of our front garden. The air has a bitter feel and it pricks sharply at my nose and fingers. I should have put my gloves on.

We walk in silence for a bit. Along a craggy path that the children like, heading out towards the cliffs. The views are truly spectacular. It's quiet aside from the low howls of the breeze in the deep valleys. It can sound dreadful sometimes and I remember being frightened the first winter I heard it. Before I knew what it was, not an animal or a person, wailing in pain.

He says, 'I think it's over, Philly.' His gruff voice breaking into my thoughts.

I feel an inward sigh of relief. Over. Perhaps he'd found a job, or perhaps he's just started to feel better.

I say, 'That's wonderful, Jim.' Hearing the smile in my voice as I reach to gently touch his hand.

He stops walking for a moment and so do I. He stares at me. Wipes a hand across his face and murmurs. 'Christ.'

He starts walking again and I follow. My hands dug deep into the insufficient pockets of my awful coat. The kids joke that it looks like a sleeping bag and the bloody thing does too. But it is warm. I rush to keep up. My two steps for every one of his. I look at his socked and sandalled feet. Wonder again if he might be cold.

'Not the depression. Though that's lifting, did a while ago to be honest.'

'Oh?'

'Us, Philly. We're over.'

Still walking. Still I am rushing to keep up with him. Then the thoughts clamour in. Large swooping things in big packs, a swarm of awful carnivorous vultures. Then little single ones. Pecking at my brain.

Over.

Us.

'What do you mean?'

'Oh come on.'

Still I can't make sense. Can't grip the intention. Inside I am watching my life slip away like water I am trying to grip between my fingers.

'Come on what?'

He stops. The howls rise from below as we stand on the cliff edge. He with his back to the wilds out there. Me facing him. Hands dug deep.

'You must know.'

'Know what?' I'm not intentionally sounding dumb. I'm tired. Exhausted from another week in my boring, soul-destroying job. Feet aching from rushing around the shops.

'Us. Philly.' He waves a hand around. He'd always been a big one for gesticulation.

He laughs. 'We've not been happy for, well, years.'

'Haven't we?'

'Of course not.'

'Oh.'

'I mean why do you think it's hit me so hard? You have no idea what it's like. Losing your place. The things you're good at.'

I think of my predicted first all those years ago. My tutor's sad face when I told him, head held high that I wouldn't be finishing just then. The girls in my office. Starting out fresh-faced, swollen with all of the promise ahead. I don't speak though. I feel weird. Drunk almost.

'Then I get home to... what? You.' He says it like an insult, and I flinch. 'And what do we have in common? Me with my career and the life I've had.' He shrugs.

'I raised the children.'

He sighs. 'And you did a good job, love but you're not the most exciting person are you? And I... well...'

Love.

Philly.

I blink once, twice. Take a step towards him. I don't know why.

He takes one back.

I ask, 'Is there someone else?'

And when he looks away, wistful almost, I have my answer.

I say, 'But when?' thinking of him, just a head in a bed. Covers pulled up to his chin.

'Carly, from the office. She kept on checking in on me.'

'Right.'

'We've been meeting. For a few months now.'

Whilst I put piles of paper into alphabetical order. Stick coloured dots on them for reference.

Things become clear. Like waking up from a dream. He's lived a very different life to mine. Separate. Always very separate. I say, 'She wasn't the first.'

Not a question. He looks away again. Shrugs. 'A man has needs. It can't just be work.'

'We had a family.'

He sighs. 'Just more work for me. I mean you could hardly blame me for not coming back between big clients and all.' He does that hand waving thing again.

I shake my head. 'Do the children know?'

'No.'

'Right.'

'We'll have to tell them—that we're splitting up—but they don't need details.'

I don't say anything.

'I saw an estate agent today.'

'Oh.'

He nods. 'We'll get you a little rental. I don't mind putting a year down for you. Until you get yourself back on your feet.'

On my feet.

A rental.

I say, 'I'll buy my own place. Once we've sold.'

He frowns. 'How will you do that?'

'What?'

'Without meaning to be rude, Philly. It's my house.'

I shake my head. As much to try and clear it as in any sort of disagreement.

He says 'Be fair, love. I worked my arse off to pay for the place. It was only ever yours if something happened to me. So the kids would be ok. But now, in this scenario, it's mine.'

He is smiling at me as though I am extremely stupid. I take another step towards him and he takes one back.

◆ ◆ ◆

It happened very quickly. In his attempt to get away from me he lost his footing and slid on the stones at the edge. He went down and all I could see were his hands clenched on a bit of broken fencing.

They'd put it along the entire edge. But it was ineffectual even when new. Just a marker rather than a barrier. He was hanging I realised, clung to a long spiralled bit of it. His voice said, 'God, Philly. Grab my hand.'

I jumped into action. It must have been less than a second because as I lay down, leaning forward, reaching for him, I saw his sandal bumping its way down the sharp edges into the cavernous rockfaces below.

I murmured, 'You should have worn trainers.' And his pale terrified face turned into a scowl.

'Come on.' His voice was high, desperate.

I grasped the other end of what was once fence, feeling splinters in my hand.

I lost my grip and he snapped, 'Can't you get anything fucking right?'

And then... I just let go.

I stood, brushing my hands on the denim of my jeans beneath the stupid sleeping-bag coat.

He said, 'Philly.' In outrage first. Then there was a cracking sound and he said my name again, strangled this time. I turned and started walking back to the house. I ignored the sounds that mingled with the howling wind.

The children were sad in their own way though none of them had been close to Jim. It was terrible of course but no-one was surprised. He'd had such an awful year after all.

And do you know it did turn out to be a lovely Christmas.

N.J. Mackay

N.J. Mackay studied Performing Arts at the BRIT School, and it turned out she wasn't very good at acting but quite liked writing scripts. She holds a BA (Hons) in English Literature and Drama, and won a full scholarship for her MA in Journalism. She is the author of two books featuring P.I. Madison Attallee, *I, Witness* and *The Lies We Tell*. Her last novel *Found Her* is a standalone psychological thriller and *The Girls Inside* will be published in February 2021. She is one third of the true-crime podcast 'Crime Girl Gang' and is represented by Hattie Grunewald at The Blair Partnership. Find her on Twitter @NikiMackayBooks, or on her website www.nikimackay.com. For more books by Niki, go to her Amazon author page: bit.ly/NJMAmazon.

THE VIGILANTE

Clare Empson

From: absolutelyfabulous@periodcostumehire.com
To: davidwinter@hotmail.com
Subject: The Victorian frock coat

Dear Mr Winter,

I hesitate in firing off this, my fourth email in as many weeks, to request return of the frock coat hired on 28th October. I ask myself if there is any point simply communing with the ether?

Yet I am perplexed to understand why you would not return it.

I am sure you are aware of the daily £5 fine for late return and the fact you already owe Period Costume Hire £135.

I believe you hired the coat to impersonate Charles Dickens for a fancy-dress party.

As I recall you were in awe of his 'visionary philanthropy'.

I ask you now to consider this question. Given the fact that Period Costume Hire is a small business, a labour of love with a miniscule turnover, which can ill afford to lose its stock, ask yourself this, Mr Winter. What would Charles do?

Yours,
Alicia Wilkinson

◆ ◆ ◆

The frock coat, a frayed thing of thick black silk, hung between two of Ella's dresses, the swirling pink and green Ralph Lauren worn at her thirtieth birthday party, and a sombre black number with a floppy white collar, which he had christened the Nun's Dress. (She looked nothing like a nun in it, particularly when she removed her tights but kept on the thigh high boots.) Sometimes he took the frock coat out of the cupboard and sat on the bed with it stretched across his lap. He fingered its soft lapels and loose third button and waited for its fumes, growing fainter each day, to reach his nostrils. Dust and stale tobacco and, perhaps, a microcosm of Ella's perfume. Every time the frock coat sent him on a journey of imagining.

◆ ◆ ◆

The stiff white card had arrived in the post.

Joe and Daisy's joint 30th at Syon House. Dress code: Literary heroes.

There was no question about whom David should be, he had been obsessed with Charles Dickens since boyhood. By the age of fifteen he had read all of his novels, weaned on his hero's quest for social justice, his mind a colourscape of workhouses, fallen women and destitute old servants. He still saw the world through Dickens' lens, the tower block slums with their cut-price cladding, the sex traffickers, the one percenters, the hedge fund fucking managers.

For Ella, the choice could be narrowed to two equally critical contenders, Virginia Woolf and Sylvia Plath. Woolf or Plath? Virginia or Sylvia, dropped waist or nipped in, bun or bangs? Virginia won in the end, mostly for her prophetic feminism, her raging against the patriarchy, but also because she went better with Charles, so well, in fact, that the frock coat and the mint green silk dress had ended up in a tangle on the floor moments before their taxi was due to arrive. It was Virginia's stockings that had done it; Ella, a purist, had insisted on buying an old school suspender belt from the Queen's lingerie suppliers and it had tipped him over the edge.

◆ ◆ ◆

They were late for the party but that hadn't mattered.

'So what if we miss the champagne?' Ella had said, kissing him hard in the back of the taxi. 'I hate champagne, it gives me a headache.'

It was a warm, pinkish late autumn evening and it seemed as if nothing could go wrong.

The guests were still pooling in front of the house when they arrived, a carpet bag mix of Hawaiian shirts (Hunter S), white ruffs (William S) and too many Jane Austens. The splendour of Syon House that night. They dined on oysters and rare roast beef in the gallery, a thin corridor of a room that was made even more gorgeous with candlelight and where, apparently, Lady Jane Grey was offered the crown. Ella had revealed this bit of information in an underground hiss; they tried to shield their bookishness from the public eye. After dinner, while everyone else drifted outside to smoke cigarettes or drink cocktails, David and Ella remained in the gallery. They sat together on a gilt bench upholstered in rose pink velvet and allowed Lady Jane Grey to join them. David was a history teacher but the job description did not summate his passion for the past. Simply he dwelled in it, the centuries rolling back, traffic disappearing, streets narrowing, urchins and potmen and match girls forming in front of his eyes. It was his secret gift and in Ella he had found a life partner who was happy to time travel with him.

◆ ◆ ◆

When the party ended, they bypassed the taxi queue and kept on walking. David had told Ella about their proximity to the former Tukes mental asylum and she had worn flat brogues specially.

'Then we must go and see it, Davey.'

They stood in front of the Palladian house and concluded that, as asylums go, this one was rather lovely with its arched windows, domed roof and Doric columns. The fact that Charles had tried to have his wife Catherine committed when she had nothing wrong with her aside from the withering of age, was deeply distressing to David. This had been hinted at and suspected for years but several months ago a letter had come to light confirming that, yes indeed, Charles Dickens, social justice commentator and campaigner, had attempted to get his wife locked up so he could continue banging his mistress with impunity. It had upset David more than he let on, this midlife transgression of Dickens. But Ella understood.

'He was mad with love, we must let him off,' Ella said, capturing David's hand and pressing it against the bumpiness of her authentic suspender belt and it is here, to this exact moment, that he chose to return each night.

◆ ◆ ◆

From: absolutelyfabulous@periodcostumehire.com
To: davidwinter@hotmail.com
Subject: The Victorian frock coat

Dear Mr Winter,

The Christmas party rush is on, plenty of people who wish to be Dickens for a night but I imagine you know that.

I thought it might be helpful to tell you a little bit more about the coat's provenance.

It belonged to a friend of mine, or rather, to be exact, to his great grandfather.

My friend found it packed away in a trunk in the attic, reeking of camphor, but otherwise immaculately preserved, a relic from the nineteenth century.

It was generous of him to bring me the coat, knowing my fastidiousness for all things authentic, a predilection I suspect we share.

So yes, this coat would have been rubbing shoulders with the great and good of London society around the same time your man Dickens was wearing his.

I have a question for you, Mr Winter.

What would Charles do?

Yours,
Alicia Wilkinson

◆ ◆ ◆

In the sixth week of the frock coat's captivity, David tried it on. He wore it with his pinstripe wedding trousers and polished black Oxfords, which still bore the mud and dark splodges of that night. Like David, Dickens was an insomniac but he had turned his sleeplessness to good use with his night-time prowls around the city. David thought he would do the same. The air felt cool but the coat was warm with its thick lining made of felt. David was both oblivious and observant as he walked through Fulham Broadway, impervious to second glances but with an acute awareness that was like a direct line into the hearts of strangers. He knew the frantically smoking couple outside the Sports Bar were on the verge of breaking up though they might easily have been on a catastrophic date. On Dawes Road he understood the young girl who was walking ten feet ahead of him had missed her night bus and decided to chance the street. In the stiffness of her neck, the quickening of her step, he read her uneasiness. David knew to tail her from a distance, not close enough to cause alarm, but within reach of any unfolding emergency. He was buoyed by the task, momentarily transported by a mission that made him feel connected, useful.

'Are you following me?'

They had travelled half a mile peaceably and now the girl had stopped and spun around, a surprising staccato movement that made him think of the game Grandmother's Footsteps.

'Escorting from a safe distance,' David said.

'What?'

The girl's face was twisted into a scowl.

'Just in case you needed help.'

'Leave me alone, you ponce.'

From: absolutelyfabulous@periodcostumehire.com
To: davidwinter@hotmail.com
Subject: The Victorian frock coat

Dear Mr Winter,

You now owe the shop £240 for the late return of the Victorian frock coat.

I find myself wondering why you are unable to return it.

Two possibilities spring to mind.

You could have died (far be it from me to wish such a tragedy upon you). But as the carefree young man who hired the frock coat back in October exuded health and happiness, gladly I discount this theory.

Or you are simply too lazy to make the journey to my shop.

Again, this does not make any sense. I pride myself on my ability to assess character and you are not a lazy man, Mr Winter.

I remind you of your hero's honourability and request that you ask yourself this.

What would Charles do?

Yours,
Alicia Wilkinson

◆ ◆ ◆

He saw many things on his nightly wanders. The homeless (or houseless as Dickens called them): girls, boys, middle-aged women, old men, stuffed into doorways, foreheads jutting out from sleeping bags. Once or twice he thought about stopping for a chat; he wanted to but couldn't quite pluck up the courage. Instead he was careful to say 'good night' as he passed and he always gave money, whatever he had on him, twenty pounds one time. Ella had firm views on how the homeless should be treated (firm views on everything). It was one of the few things they had disagreed on. When they were first together, he'd walked past a boy begging outside Leicester Square tube. He couldn't have been more than fifteen.

'If we give him cash, he'll spend it on drugs,' he'd told her, low voiced. 'Let's get him something to eat from Costa.'

More times than he could count, he spied a homeless person from the warmth of a café and he never failed to set down something good to eat beside them. But Ella had run back to the boy with the contents of her purse and, when she rejoined David, she had furious tears in her eyes.

'If it was me, I'd want all the drugs.'

◆ ◆ ◆

He saw new couples on the streets, young and hopeful and a little silly, just as they had been at the beginning. He was becoming an expert at recognising the ones on a first date, he read it in their shall-we-shan't we gait, closer together than friends, not yet as close as the lovers who kissed passionately on the tube each morning as if to continue something that had begun the night before. Sometimes he was witness to a first kiss, he always turned away but not before the proximity to romance broke him up a bit. He and Ella had had the most perfect date, six years ago now. He'd instructed her to meet him outside Bethnal Green tube station, determined to keep their destination secret until the last possible moment. David could remember exactly how he felt when he spied her walking out of the exit, that lurching sensation, like vertigo. She was wearing a bright blue duffel coat and a bobble hat made from arran wool and he'd thought, Ali McGraw in *Love Story*. She held out her hand to him straight away and they walked towards the green, sealed and seamless, no shall-we-shan't-we awkwardness for them. And as they turned into Cambridge Heath Road, she froze suddenly and clapped her hands together (no sound, she was wearing knitted gloves).

'I knew it. We're going to the Museum of Childhood, aren't we? It was my mother's favourite place.'

Ella's mother had died when she was eleven and she still missed her. It was the second thing she'd told him. First thing, 'I have a problem with modernity. I don't really fit with this life.'

'Me too,' he'd said, and their futures spliced.

◆ ◆ ◆

From: absolutelyfabulous@periodcostumehire.com
To: davidwinter@hotmail.com
Subject: The Victorian frock coat

Dear Mr Winter,

I find myself worrying about you at the oddest times, often in the middle of the night.

I can't shake the feeling that perhaps something has happened to you?

If you've read my emails, you will understand why I can't give up on the frock coat.

I can't quite give up on you either.

Yours,
Alicia Wilkinson

◆ ◆ ◆

David had lived in the capital all these years without knowing its secrets. At night the city filled with a disparate people, ghost hunters and bat watchers, vagrants and drunks. The jet lagged and the lonely. The streets ran with rivulets of emotion not seen in the light. And there was unity in their rooflessness. Sometimes the coat provoked comments as he glided past —'weirdo' 'psycho' 'nutjob'—but David scarcely heard them. He was imperturbable, caught between two worlds. Ethereal otherness was his chosen state.

The coat had become his superpower and whenever he wore it he could avert disaster. Not for himself, never that, but for everyone else. He was afraid of nothing when he intervened in a couple's fight on a corner of Leicester Square. The woman thanked him, the man punched him. And David liked it, the bruise that bloomed the following morning was a badge of honour. There were so many situations in the capital requiring an insuperable man in a frock coat. A disorientated old lady in a nightdress needed escorting home. A bunch of schoolboys smacking the life out of each other for kicks needed the sternness and frankly, freakiness, of the Dickensian figure who was frightened of no one.

◆ ◆ ◆

And then the Friday night before Christmas arrived. What was it with Christmas? Why did everyone use it as an excuse to become paralytically drunk when it was—supposedly—the chosen birthday for Jesus? He arrived in Soho in the early hours of Saturday morning, the streets thronged with drunks. Outside a pub a waif like girl was projectiling a neat pile of vomit. He tried to assist but was warned away by her torrent of profanity. David was being vacuumed towards the red and gold restaurant where he had proposed to Ella. After the proposal, he and Ella made a point of eating at Rules once a month—usually on pay day—and the waiters gave them their favourite table whenever they could. Beef Wellington and salmon en croûte. Minted garden peas. Steamed ginger pudding with crème anglaise to share. Their order rarely changed.

◆ ◆ ◆

He was only a street or two away from the restaurant when a scream fractured the air. A short, curtailed cry that led him backwards through the days and weeks and months to a place where a man and woman were standing outside an asylum. Chiswick. Dickens. Ella. Tonight, in the shadows, he saw a girl on the ground, a man crouched down beside her and a boy sprinting away, incongruous with the long hair that flew out from beneath his beanie, the raspberry pink bag under his arm. All these months of walking ten or twelve miles a night had given him a new fitness. This boy was fast but David was faster. He was almost abreast with him when the boy stopped, turned around and lunged at David; the blade he held was long and piratical, a warrior's knife. David waited for blankness but none came. The knife was caught between the outer layer and the thick felt lining of his coat. The boy wrested it free and made to lunge again but David grabbed his wrist and squeezed hard until he cried out. Where did this strength come from, this rage? He felt he could crush his wrist bones into dust.

'Drop the knife.'

It was his stern history teacher's voice and he felt the boy's fingers distend, the knife clattering to the ground.

'What kind of freak are you?' the boy hissed.

David looked into his face for one moment before he ran off and what he saw, several layers down, was torment. Another night, another soul. David stooped to pick up the knife and hid it in his inside pocket, cool air rushing through the slashes of his coat. There was a destination to this journey now and at last he had understood it. Had Dickens felt the same the night he started out at Waterloo Bridge, passing by the Theatre Royal and the Bank of England before he wound up outside Bedlam, pondering on the parallels between the insane and those who dreamed wildly in their beds? He thought about his accomplices on the street. The pigeon feeder in Trafalgar Square who had babbled at the birds and nodded when David told her he was Charles Dickens as if this was nothing more than she expected. The drug-dazed boy in Highgate who claimed he had been at a party singing a duet with Elton John ('Don't Go Breaking My Heart'). They were all equals in the landscape of the lost.

◆ ◆ ◆

David found himself on Chelsea Bridge, a part of London he tried hard to avoid. He took the knife from his coat and dropped it into the river. He stood on that bridge, peering down into the dappling water, for a long time. Night had all but drifted from the sky and David was ready to cross to the other side. When he first met Ella, she lived in a mansion flat on Prince of Wales Drive. They had drunk tea in the shabby pale green drawing room with its floor to ceiling windows overlooking the park. Standing in front of York Mansions, he conjured up an image of Ella in a cream beret and bright blue coat coming out of the front door. It was so good to see her, this younger version of his wife. His sadness was intense and glorious as he walked through the gates to the park—with Ella, and also without her.

David was drawn towards the glint of the Peace Pagoda in nearby Battersea Park, a place where they had once picnicked on brie sandwiches and bottles of fizzy water while boats coasted up and down the river and behind them, the air filled with the shouts of children. The laziness of that afternoon, scarcely bothering to talk when there was so much they might have said, the two of them reckless with their vision of infinity.

The sky had begun its transformation, grey became a fine, pale pink with hints of gold. As he drew closer to the pagoda, David heard the slow and measured beating of a drum. He felt no surprise when he found an elderly man in orange robes sitting cross legged in front of the famous gold buddha, a circle of sun worshippers around him. This was what his life had become, an imperceptible horizon where dreams bled into reality with the illusory power of enchantment. David sat down with them and listened to their chant, words that became fluid and shapeless as the minutes passed, melding into one long meandering sound. He felt it like a vibration in his bones, his bloodstream, his heart. David turned his head to gaze at the stretch of dark water beside him, at London briefly dipped in pink and gold. A place of palaces and monks and pigeon feeders and boys who buried their despair beneath savagery. It was his city. Where he belonged. His head began to fill with a chant of his own.

Mad with love mad with love mad with love. Those were his words and he said them over and over, sent them up and out into the burning ether. He closed his eyes and felt the sun warming him as it rose. There was just one more thing to do.

◆ ◆ ◆

He arrived at Period Costume Hire at exactly nine-thirty and found it already open, Alicia Wilkinson sitting behind her desk. She looked up as he stepped through the door and smiled.

'There you are,' she said as if she had been expecting him.

She didn't comment on the state of the coat, knife ripped and filthy, mocked, scorned and grieved in.

'Please,' she gestured to the chair opposite her.

David looked around the little shop with its white painted wooden floor and the rails of bright clothes, harem pants squashed in beside hooped gowns, a silken cascade of fantasy.

The last time he had been here he'd been happy.

'You stopped sending emails,' he said.

'Yes. I did a bit of digging. I was curious about you.'

Alicia opened up a drawer in her desk and removed a photocopy of a newspaper cutting. She slid it towards him, face up. A great exhaustion folded itself over David. He was at the end of his journey.

He reached out to smooth his fingers across Ella's face, a

photograph taken on her thirtieth birthday, in a dress of swirling pink and green.

He could not avoid the stark black lettering of the headline.

Hit and run driver kills woman in Chiswick

'It was my fault.'

'I doubt that,' Alicia said, but her voice was soft and measured, unlike his friends who rushed to extinguish every single 'what if', his endless, unbearable remorse. David saw that Alicia would wait.

'It was my idea to go and look at the old asylum. We could have gone home after the party like everyone else. I'd walked up the road to see if I could find a cab. And that's when a car lost control and hit the kerb. I heard her cry, the sound as the car hit her and I couldn't do anything. Thirty seconds earlier and it would have been me.'

'Is that what you wish? That you'd died?'

David bowed his head.

'I wish it hadn't been her.'

It was so simple when he put it like that. This was everything really. It wasn't that he wanted to die; more that, without Ella, he had forgotten how to live. Him and a whole nightscape of wretched beings whose lives had stopped working. Thousands of them out there on the streets at night with their heartbreak, their sorrow and pain.

'She was so—good. Why did it have to be her?'

'You seem like a good person, David.'

'Hardly. Look at this coat I've kept all this time. I'll pay you back, of course.'

Alicia laughed and then David did, the shocked reluctant laughter of a man who had almost forgotten how.

'Bloody Charles Dickens. It's his fault. If he hadn't been so hell-bent on locking up his wife in a loony bin just so he could carry on copulating with his mistress.'

There was a pause while Alicia looked at David. It felt as if she was communing whole paragraphs to him with her eyes.

'Seems to me that you need to forgive Charles Dickens,' she said and he understood she meant something quite other.

He needed to forgive himself.

'Think you can do that?'

'I can try.'

He stood up.

'I guess I should go home. I should sleep.'

'Good idea.'

'Oh, I almost forgot.'

He laughed again and began to remove the frock coat but Alicia put out one hand to halt him.

'David?'

One final gaze between them, the lovelorn widower and the woman who owned a fancy-dress shop.

'Charles would want you to keep the coat.'

Clare Empson

Clare Empson spent the first half of her career working as a national newspaper journalist before publishing her debut psychological thriller *Him* in 2018. Her second novel *Mine* was published in 2019 and she is currently working on her third. Clare lives in Wiltshire with her husband and three children. Find her on Twitter @clareempson2 or on her website: www.clareempson.com. For more books by Clare, go to her Amazon author page: bit.ly/ClareEAmazon.

HUNTED

Victoria Selman

'R*un for your life... I meant what I said...'*

That creepy Beatles song is a soundtrack in my head as I stumble, tripping against a rock half hidden in the undergrowth. I stub my toe, twist my ankle, curse softly beneath my breath. No way I want to draw attention to myself out here. No way I want to advertise my injury to him.

I push myself up, quick as I can, ignoring the throbbing in my ankle. There's blood on my jeans, so much blood. Brown and crusted. Seeing it makes my heart beat faster. If that's possible.

Where is he?

I listen for a giveaway sound; acorns crunching, the rustle of leaves. A clue as to where he might be hiding. My head's cocked, my eyes darting. Every muscle taut and primed. Yet it's difficult to hear anything over the sound of my kettledrum heart, my ragged breath.

I run every day, always follow the same ritual. Hydrate, stretches and then I'm off; all the way down to Christmas Common and back again.

There was no time for a warm-up routine this morning though, and I've run a hell of lot further than I normally do.

The sweat is dripping between my breasts and shoulder blades. My mouth is dry, a stabbing pain under my ribcage. No amount of training could have prepared me for this. For what's at stake.

Where is he?

I'm panting, flooded with adrenaline, as the wind hisses and the bony oaks watch on. Spectators to the fight.

I twist my head, left then right. I can't see him but I know he's out here. Old Crazy Eyes, so like my father with his red lumberjack shirt, bruised fists and bloodshot peepers. A drunk. A sadist.

He's hiding, lurking, waiting for his chance. Waiting to...

Crack.

A twig snaps, followed by the unmistakable gallop of feet. The sound reverberates through the forest, bouncing off the worn and weathered bark.

A rush of heat surges through me and I'm off again. I'm exhausted, wounded, and yet the need to survive pushes me on. I can't let him get...

As I tear through the trees, I think of the past week, the cabin I was confined to. The torture chamber.

I see again the wooden table in the centre of the room, blotchy with old blood; the brown patches forming interconnected shapes like countries on a map. Countries no-one in their right mind would want to visit.

I see the knives and saws and hatchets hanging on ceiling hooks. The blades polished, sharp, glinting in the light. A threat. A promise.

I see the green surgeon's apron with its long elasticated sleeves. The mask. The blue latex gloves.

And I see his wide wild eyes, inches from mine. I smell his dirty pork breath. His stale sweat.

The rattle of the hooks as the first knife is chosen, then...

My muscles tighten. An electric charge shoots down my spine. My already thundering heart doubles its efforts, smashing against my chest; a break for freedom.

He's close. I must hurry.

Hopeless, says the voice inside my head. *No point fighting it...*

His voice.

How many times did he say those words? How many times did he raise his fist, his knife?

Stop it, I tell myself. *Don't think of that now.*

If only I knew where he was.

I keep running.

Thorny bushes reach out their arms to block my path. Hidden roots trip me up.

My face is scratched, my throat parched. When the rain comes, cold and heavy, I stick out my tongue but it doesn't quench my thirst. The water will have to wait.

Where is he?

Chest heaving, I scan the area.

An animal flits out of the bushes. For a moment I think it's him. And then I see a flash of colour through the leaves. His shirt, the same red-orange hue as fresh blood.

He's off again and so am I; breathing air in through my nose and out through my mouth, arching my toes up towards my shins to quicken my cadence. Lengthening my strides.

The gap between us starts to narrow. I can actually smell him now, an animal scent. Vulpine. Foul. He looks over his shoulder and stumbles, and I think it's going to be okay. That this is my chance.

I'm wrong.

We've reached a road. How did I not see that?

The light is different here, the shadows have melted away. And then I hear it; the unmistakable rumble of an approaching engine.

My throat closes up. My veins fill with lead.

Of all the miserable luck!

A police car, can you believe? Decked out with tinsel, Christmas carols blasting out the open window.

It's slowing. My quarry's waving the driver down, arms moving as if wiping steam from a mirror.

The car stops. A copper gets out, puts his hand on Crazy Eyes' shoulder, his own eyes widening in horror as the bastard tells his tale.

It won't take them long to find the cabin. The chamber where I was tortured as a child and where I now torture men who remind me of my abuser. Stand-ins for the monster death stole from me. My father. The devil.

They'll find the cabin first. And then the graves. All six of them.

But will they find me?

In an instant the game has changed.

I take one last look at the car then bolt.

Now it's me running for my life.

Victoria Selman

Victoria Selman has an MA in Modern History from the University of Oxford and studied Creative Writing at the City Lit. She writes opinion pieces for the *Independent* and co-hosts *Crime Girl Gang,* a true crime podcast in which three crime writers examine cold cases and then solve them from a fictional perspective.

She is the Amazon Charts bestselling author of the Ziba MacKenzie criminal profiler series. Her debut novel, *Blood For Blood* was shortlisted for the 2017 CWA Debut Dagger Award and has had over half a million eBook downloads. Find her on Twitter @VictoriaSelman, or at www.victoriaselmanauthor.com. For more books by Victoria, go to her Amazon author page: bit.ly/VictoriaSAmazon.

BLOODY CHRISTMAS

Harriet Tyce

The camel in the front row is crying because one of the donkeys has kicked it in the shin. Two of the sheep are scuffling, ears wagging as they try and punch each other without anyone noticing. The angel second to the left looks as if she's about to punch someone, too. Nothing beatific about her expression.

'What part is she playing?'

He looks at me with complete scorn. 'Mary. You know that.'

'Oh yes. Sorry.' I do remember, now. He's done a lovely job with the outfit. He told me all about it, while I tried to research sentencing law for aggravated burglary times three.

I pull my phone out of my bag. I'm meant to be in chambers, in a conference I had to cancel last minute. Now he jabs my arm, jaw tense. Fuck's sake. I put the phone away.

They're all on stage now, overflowing to the front. Twenty sheep, twenty donkeys, twenty camels, twenty alpacas. Alpacas.

'Since when were there fucking alpacas in a nativity play?'

'Shhh,' he hisses between his teeth. A woman in the row in front turns round and glares at me.

It's getting hot. The hall's packed, festive animals and all their respective parents and guardians. I can feel sweat breaking out on my forehead, my cheeks flushing red. I want to take my scarf off but I can't. I thought I was OK earlier but I was still drunk. It's wearing off now. I can feel the alcohol oozing out of my skin, heat building up through my body. The scarf's wound tightly and it's constricting me, cutting off the flow of blood to my head.

I try to reason with myself, tell myself I'm not being strangled, but it feels tighter and tighter. I pull at the top of it, easing a little away from my neck. Not too much. I can't let it slip. If he sees my neck... it seemed so funny last night. Less so now.

I can't breathe. I'm starting to panic, my heart beating faster and faster, the toxins breaking down inside me. There's acid building up in my stomach, my oesophagus burning. I know I need to get out, get some fresh air, cool down. If only I could take this fucking scarf off. I look along the row of people. We're sitting right at the end, next to the wall. I'll have to disturb so many of them if I try and leave. My agitation grows as I pull at my scarf and look around me, trying to see if there's any way of escape. None.

The children are singing now. I think it's meant to be 'O Little Town of Bethlehem' but it's so discordant it's impossible to tell. Someone is playing a piano, the top notes slightly out of tune, and the cacophony is ceaseless. It's working its way into my head, the pounding intensifying at the front of my skull. He grabs my arm, *look, look, there she is, our little girl,* a small figure in blue marching across the stage, but I can feel the acid climbing inexorably up my chest, my neck, and my mouth is starting to water, all the tell-tale signs that I'm going to vomit.

A child narrator is lisping its way through Herod's order that all people must return to their place of birth and Mary and Joseph are being turned away by an infant innkeeper but by now I've jumped up and I'm pushing my way along the row, hand firmly over mouth as the puke threatens to burst out. I know they're pissed off, the mutterings growing around me, the narration faltering on stage, and I can't look at her standing up there, my little Mary, resplendent in her pillowcase, I don't want to see the confusion on her face as I flee to the back of the hall and beyond.

The loo isn't far, and I make it just in time, kneeling on the floor as I retch and retch. A gush of liquid, the water I'd necked so optimistically, the black coffees, a vile dark sludge from the red wine I drank so liberally in the restaurant last night, splatters hitting the basin of the lavatory, splashing back in my face. Finally it's all out, and with the cubicle door locked safely behind me, I pull off my scarf, desperate to feel cool air at my throat. I slump on my heels, head against the loo seat, rubbing my fingers along my neck, trying to feel the edges of the massive purple mark left on my throat.

◆ ◆ ◆

'Is that what you're wearing?' he said the night before. I'd scrambled to get home in time to put her to bed, read her a story and glam up for the chambers Christmas night out.

'Why?'

'I dunno, I mean, I used to like it on you. But I'm not sure...'

I pulled at the garment, a wrap dress I hadn't worn for a few years. I'd lost the baby weight, though, it was looking good. At least, I thought it was.

'What's wrong with it? It fits fine.'

'As long as you're happy in it, that's the main thing.' He smiled, though it didn't reach his eyes.

'But—'

'Look, I'm not saying you shouldn't wear it. I just wonder if you don't have something that's a bit more, well, suitable.'

'Suitable for what?'

'Suitable for a work night out. It's a bit tight, I have to say. Maybe you have to accept your body shape has changed.'

'But I've lost all the weight. And it does up. I think it looks nice.' I peered more closely in the mirror – I couldn't see any problem with it at all.

'As I said, it's what you think that matters.'

I looked myself up and down once more. I didn't have time to change – it would have to do. But I was feeling uneasy, now. I thought it suited me. But maybe he was right. Maybe it didn't work. I dithered in front of the wardrobe but time was moving too fast.

'I've got to go,' I said. I walked over and reached my arms around him, kissing his cheek. He was unresponsive, his body unyielding in my arms.

'I hope you won't be late,' he said. 'It's the Nativity Play to-morrow.'

'Tomorrow? It's on Friday. It says so on the calendar. Look,' I said, pulling out my phone to show him the entry on our shared calendar.

'It's definitely tomorrow,' he said. 'I put the entry in myself.'

I looked again. He was right. It was tomorrow. Though I could have sworn it was Friday.

'I don't understand. I'd never have agreed to the dinner to-night if I'd realised.'

'I do wish you'd check things properly,' he said with a sigh.

'Well, it's too late now. Bloody Christmas. I'll just have to deal with it.'

'She's put a lot of effort into it,' he said. 'We've worked very hard on her costume, too. Don't spoil it.'

'I'm not going to spoil it,' I said. 'I'll make it work.'

I sat on the bus down to Holborn, guilt clawing at my insides. It didn't stop until I'd had my first drink, the wine smoothing it all away. Everyone was out at the restaurant, the conversation upbeat, cheerful. The wine flowed freely all evening, my glass never empty. I talked to my friends, to the clerks, to the pupils. People laughed at my jokes. I didn't check my phone – I didn't want to know.

Later we went to a club, a basement somewhere around Soho, a place I'd never find sober. There were more lawyers there, solicitors and barristers. A popular night for Christmas parties, the middle Thursday of December, the floor heaving with white-shirted men necking lager and shouting over the music.

That's when I saw him. Standing at the bar. As dark and brooding as ever. Clive Owen. Or as near as dammit. We'd only met a couple of times before, when I did a mention of his for someone else in chambers, and when I'd bumped into him in the corridor at the Old Bailey. Both times I'd been very aware of him, imagining almost I could feel his heat radiating towards me. Now he was watching me as I walked over, a smile curving up one side of his mouth.

'Fancy seeing you here,' he said, leaning in close. 'I wouldn't have thought you'd end up in a place like this.'

'It's not that bad,' I said, but I laughed, knowing it was a lie. He didn't respond, but leaned forward, ran his finger along my jaw and down my throat, over my clavicle and pausing at my breastbone, his eyebrow raised. I put my hand up, undecided whether I should push his away. I didn't.

'You look lovely,' he said. 'First time I've seen you in a dress. It suits you.'

I smiled. 'My husband didn't think so.'

'He's a fool. Can I get you a drink?'

I nodded. We drank, we danced. Too loud to talk, though he said a couple of things in my ear that made me laugh. Made me blush. Later, he leaned forward, kissed me. I nearly kissed him back, before I caught myself, pulled away. He made a face.

'Sad,' he said. 'I thought we were getting on.'

The dance floor was still busy, still buzzing, people spinning round me like balls in a roulette wheel, me and him in the still centre, his hand to my neck, then inside my dress, on my breast. I stood calm, unmoving, while the room span and span, before a black light took me and I stood on tiptoe and bit his neck before kissing him. It was a long while before he backed away, laughed.

'I knew I was right. I always know when someone's into me,' he said.

He pulled me over to the corner, a tatty armchair, pulling me onto his knee. I was young again, teenaged, at a disco with a boy I fancied. Not thirty-something with a husband and child at home. He sucked at my neck and when I pushed him off he laughed.

'Just getting you back. You bit my neck, I'm biting yours.'

Later, I went to the loo, dizzy with booze and lust, until I looked in the mirror, saw the great purple blotch he'd left on my neck. The shock of it sobered me. I could hear my daughter's voice in my head, *What's that, Mummy?* I left the loo, head down, ran out. He caught up with me on the pavement outside as I tried to hail a cab, stumbling into the night.

'Can I call you?' he said. 'I want to see you again.'

'I'm sorry, this was a mistake. I can't.' A cab stopped and I climbed in, turning my face away.

◆ ◆ ◆

Another retch, more foam spat down the pan, more retching, and finally the thin stream of yellow-green bile that means this is nearly over. I get back to my feet, flush the loo and leave the cubicle, staggering slightly as I make my way to the basin. I'd splash my face with water but I've got make up on. Or I did. Most of it has migrated down my face between sweating and puking. I wind my scarf back round my neck, making sure the love bite is hidden. It's time to go back.

By now the three kings are halfway through their adoration, gold and frankincense and myrrh. I could do with some perfuming, I think, wafts of hangover seeping off me. I look at Mary's little face, my daughter concentrating so hard on her part. My heart contracts. She deserves better.

One more hymn, a rousing cheer, and it's over. No one mentions the slaughter of the innocents. It wouldn't be tactful to point out what happened next. I stand near the hall exit, waiting for him to find me, although all I want to do is run away, dodge his disappointment, the confusion on her face.

'I can't even speak to you right now, I'm so angry,' he says. 'Why do you always let her down?'

I don't mean to, I think. *I love her. I want to be the best mother I can. But everything I do seems to fuck it up further.*

After a few minutes she runs over to us, gleaming with pride. 'Did I do OK, Mummy?' she says, and my heart contracts even further. 'I was really worried I was going to drop Jesus. But I didn't.'

'You were brilliant,' I say. Maybe she didn't realise I missed most of it. Maybe it's all right.

He nods his agreement. 'You really were. It's a shame your mum wasn't there to see it, but I thought you did great.'

She looks up at me, face full of confusion. 'But you were here. Why did you miss it?'

I'm about to explode with shame. With rage. I glare at him but his face is bland, expressionless. 'I'm sorry, sweetie. I had a sore tummy. I had to run to the loo.'

'Self-inflicted,' he says.

'What does self in... inf... mean?' she says.

'It means—' he starts, but I interrupt.

'It means that I had a sore tummy and I'm very sorry I had to miss some of it, but I thought you did brilliantly. I don't want anything to spoil that.' I reach over and pull her into a hug, glaring at him over her head. He shrugs, hands motioning a gesture of innocent confusion.

'I don't want to lie to her,' he says. 'Actions have consequences.'

I nearly punch him.

◆ ◆ ◆

At last I'm on my own. She's safely in front of the TV, watching *Frozen* for the seventeenth time. He's gone out to the clinic for his afternoon appointments, refusing to make eye contact before he leaves, his kiss goodbye to her ostentatious, underlining the absence of one to me. I sit down at my desk, papers open in front of me as I prepare for a GBH trial that's starting tomorrow, solace of a sort in someone else's misery.

I'm halfway through the medical report (unpaid debts, three fingers severed clean off with a sharpened Sabatier) when my phone pings with a message from an unfamiliar number.

Amazing arse, Alison. Let's do that again soon. And more.

Not signed. It doesn't need to be. My finger hovers over delete. I should block the number. Another ping. This time from Carl.

I will be late. Men's group tonight, as I expect you've forgotten. Do Tilly an omelette and carrot sticks – I assume that's not beyond you.

This time no hesitation. I delete Carl's message immediately, anger surging up. I type a reply telling him to go fuck himself. I delete that, too. Taking several deep breaths, I calm myself. Then I open the arse message again, reread it. Type my reply.

Hello Patrick. What exactly did you have in mind?

Harriet Tyce

Harriet Tyce was born and grew up in Edinburgh. She did a degree in English Literature at the University of Oxford before a law conversion course at City University, following which she was a criminal barrister for nearly ten years.

Having escaped law and early motherhood, she started writing, and completed the MA in Creative Writing – Crime Fiction at the University of East Anglia. Her debut novel, *Blood Orange*, was published in 2019, and was a Richard & Judy book club bestseller, as well as being shortlisted for the Dead Good Reader's Award and the Theakston's Old Peculier Crime Novel of the Year. Her second novel, *The Lies You Told*, was published in August 2020. She lives in north London with her husband and children, and two rather demanding pets, a cat and a dog. Find her on Twitter @harriet_tyce or on her website www.harriettyceauthor.com. For more books by Harriet, go to her Amazon author page: bit.ly/HarrietTAmazon.

ACKNOWLEDGEMENTS

In the Spring of 2020, in the wake of the coronavirus crisis, I teamed up with fourteen contemporary crime writers to produce *Afraid of the Light*, a short story anthology in support of the mental health charity, Samaritans.

What started off a fun project with friends born out of a desire to do something to help those battling the effects of lockdown, took off in ways none of us could have imagined.

Afraid of the Light became an Amazon bestseller, was featured in the national media and even attracted the attention of film and TV star John Sessions, who very generously offered to narrate an audiobook for us free of charge.

Little over six months later, we've teamed up again, this time with some of the biggest names in crime fiction joining us as guest authors.

We're so grateful to Val McDermid, Mark Billingham, Sophie Hannah and Harriet Tyce for lending their time and talent to help us raise money to support those suffering from domestic abuse.

Huge thanks also to the very talented Claire Ward, who designed our fabulous cover 'pro bono', to EDPR for helping us with PR activity and so kindly waiving their fee, to Pigeonhole 'The book club in your pocket' for serialising the anthology at a discounted rate and to RAK studios for generously donating studio time.

They say behind every great man is a great woman. They

should also say, behind every great writer is a great editor. In our case, this is Miranda Jewess, editor extraordinaire who has lent us her keen eye and marketing insight to make this book something we are all so proud of and taking it to a whole other level.

And finally thank you to YOU, our readers, for trusting us with your time and letting us tell you our stories. Every copy of *Afraid of the Christmas Lights* you've bought has helped women suffering from domestic violence who have never needed our support more than they do now.

If you've enjoyed the anthology, we'd be so grateful if you'd post an Amazon review and do join the chat on Twitter using the hashtag #AfraidOfTheChristmasLights.

We'd love to hear from you!

Victoria Selman
Anthology Coordinator
@Victoria Selman

AUTHOR LINKS

Mark Billingham
@MarkBillingham
www.markbillingham.com
bit.ly/MarkBAmazon

Sophie Hannah
@sophiehannahCB1
www.sophiehannah.com
bit.ly/SophieHAmazon

Kate Simants
@katesboat
bit.ly/KateSAmazon

Phoebe Morgan
@Phoebe_A_Morgan
Instagram @phoebeannmorgan
Facebook @PhoebeMorganAuthor
www.phoebemorganauthor.com
bit.ly/PhoebeMAmazon

S.R. Masters
@srmastersauthor

www.sr-masters.com
bit.ly/SRMAmazon

Adam Southward
@adamsouthward
adamsouthward.com
bit.ly/AdamSAmazon

T.E. Kinsey
@TEKinsey
Facebook www.facebook.com/tekinsey
Instagram @tekinseymysteries
www.tekinsey.uk
bit.ly/TEKAmazon

Elle Croft
@elle_croft
bit.ly/ElleCAmazon

Heather Critchlow
@h_critchlow
Instagram @heather.critchlow
www.heathercritchlow.com

James Delargy
@jdelargyauthor
bit.ly/JamesDAmazon

Jo Furniss
@Jo_Furniss
Facebook @JoFurnissAuthor
Instagram @jofurnissauthor
www.jofurniss.com
bit.ly/JoFAmazon

Robert Scragg
@robert_scragg
www.robertscragg.com
bit.ly/RobertSAmazon

Rachael Blok
@MsRachaelBlok
www.rachaelblok.com
bit.ly/RachaelBAmazon

Dominic Nolan
@NolanDom
bit.ly/DominicNAmazon

N.J. Mackay
@NikiMackayBooks
www.nikimackay.com
bit.ly/NJMAmazon

Clare Empson
@ClareEmpson2
www.clareempson.com
bit.ly/ClareEAmazon

Victoria Selman
@VictoriaSelman
www.victoriaselmanauthor.com
bit.ly/VictoriaSAmazon

Harriet Tyce
@harriet_tyce
www.harriettyceauthor.com
bit.ly/HarrietTAmazon

Printed in Great Britain
by Amazon